SEAL OF THE UNIVERSITY OF CALIFORNIA
LET THERE BE LIGHT
1868

He too saw the image in the water; but he looked up at once, and became aware of the lovely Lassie who sate there up in the tree. *Page 70*

EAST OF THE SUN AND WEST OF THE MOON

OLD TALES FROM THE NORTH

ILLUSTRATED BY
KAY NIELSEN

NEW YORK
GEORGE H DORAN COMPANY

PREFACE

A FOLK-TALE, in its primitive plainness of word and entire absence of complexity in thought, is peculiarly sensitive and susceptible to the touch of stranger hands; and he who has been able to acquaint himself with the *Norske Folkeeventyr* of Asbjörnsen and Moe (from which these stories are selected), has an advantage over the reader of an English rendering. Of this advantage Mr. Kay Nielsen has fully availed himself: and the exquisite *bizarrerie* of his drawings aptly expresses the innermost significance of the old-world, old-wives' fables. For to term these legends, Nursery Tales, would be to curtail them, by nine-tenths, of their interest. They are the romances of the childhood of Nations: they are the never-failing springs of sentiment, of sensation, of heroic example, from which primeval peoples drank their fill at will.

The quaintness, the tenderness, the grotesque yet realistic intermingling of actuality with supernaturalism, by which the original *Norske Folkeeventyr* are characterised, will make an appeal to all, as represented in the pictures of Kay Nielsen. And these imperishable traditions, whose bases are among the very roots of all antiquity, are here reincarnated in line and colour, to the delight of all who ever knew or now shall know them.

Permission to reprint the Stories in this book, which originally appeared in Sir G. W. Dasent's "Popular Tales from the Norse," has been obtained from Messrs. George Routledge & Sons, Ltd. THE THREE PRINCESSES IN THE BLUE MOUNTAIN is printed by arrangement with Messrs. David Nutt; and PRINCE LINDWORM is newly translated for this volume.

CONTENTS

ILLUSTRATIONS

EAST OF THE SUN AND WEST OF THE MOON

THE BLUE BELT

PRINCE LINDWORM

THE LASSIE AND HER GODMOTHER

THE THREE PRINCESSES OF WHITELAND

THE GIANT WHO HAD NO HEART IN HIS BODY

THE WIDOW'S SON

THE THREE PRINCESSES IN THE BLUE MOUNTAIN

"Well, mind and hold tight by my shaggy coat, and then there's nothing to fear," said the Bear, so she rode a long, long way. Page 10

EAST OF THE SUN AND WEST OF THE MOON

ONCE on a time there was a poor husbandman who had so many children that he hadn't much of either food or clothing to give them. Pretty children they all were, but the prettiest was the youngest daughter, who was so lovely there was no end to her loveliness.

So one day, 'twas on a Thursday evening late at the fall of the year, the weather was so wild and rough outside, and it was so cruelly dark, and rain fell and wind blew, till the walls of the cottage shook again. There they all sat round the fire, busy with this thing and that. But just then, all at once something gave three taps on the window-pane. Then the father went out to see what was the matter; and, when he got out of doors, what should he see but a great big *White Bear*.

"Good-evening to you!" said the *White Bear*.

"The same to you!" said the man.

"Will you give me your youngest daughter? If you will, I'll make you as rich as you are now poor," said the *Bear*.

Well, the man would not be at all sorry to be so rich; but still he thought he must have a bit of a talk with his daughter first; so he went in and told them how there was a great *White Bear* waiting outside, who had given his word to make them so rich if he could only have the youngest daughter.

The lassie said "No!" outright. Nothing could get her to say anything else; so the man went out and settled it with the *White Bear* that he should come again the next Thursday evening and get an answer. Meantime he talked his daughter over, and kept on telling her of all the riches they would get, and how well off she would be herself; and so at last she thought better of it, and washed and mended her rags, made herself as smart as she could, and was ready to start. I can't say her packing gave her much trouble.

Next Thursday evening came the *White Bear* to fetch her, and she got upon his back with her bundle, and off they went. So, when they had gone a bit of the way, the *White Bear* said:

"Are you afraid?"

"No," she wasn't.

"Well! mind and hold tight by my shaggy coat, and

then there's nothing to fear," said the *Bear*.

So she rode a long, long way, till they came to a great steep hill. There, on the face of it, the *White Bear* gave a knock, and a door opened, and they came into a castle where there were many rooms all lit up; rooms gleaming with silver and gold; and there, too, was a table ready laid, and it was all as grand as grand could be. Then the *White Bear* gave her a silver bell; and when she wanted anything, she was only to ring it, and she would get it at once.

Well, after she had eaten and drunk, and evening wore on, she got sleepy after her journey, and thought she would like to go to bed, so she rang the bell; and she had scarce taken hold of it before she came into a chamber where there was a bed made, as fair and white as any one would wish to sleep in, with silken pillows and curtains and gold fringe. All that was in the room was gold or silver; but when she had gone to bed and put out the light, a man came and laid himself alongside her. That was the *White Bear*, who threw off his beast shape at night; but she never saw him, for he always came after she had put out the light, and before the day dawned he was up and off again. So things went on happily for a while, but at last she began to get silent and sorrowful; for there she went about all day alone, and she longed to go home to see her father and mother and brothers and sisters. So one day, when the *White Bear* asked what it was that she lacked, she said it was so dull and lonely there, and how she longed to go home to see her father and mother and brothers and sisters, and that was why she was so sad and sorrowful, because she couldn't get to them.

"Well, well!" said the *Bear*, "perhaps there's a cure for all this; but you must promise me one thing, not to talk alone with your mother, but only when the rest are by to hear; for she'll take you by the hand and try to lead you into a room alone to talk; but you must mind and not do that, else you'll bring bad luck on both of us."

So one Sunday the *White Bear* came and said, now they could set off to see her father and mother. Well, off they started, she sitting on his back; and they went far and long. At last they came to a grand house, and there her brothers and sisters were running about out of doors at play, and everything was so pretty, 'twas a joy to see.

"This is where your father and mother live now," said the *White Bear*; "but don't forget what I told you, else you'll make us both unlucky."

"No! bless her, she'd not forget;"—and when she had reached the house, the *White Bear* turned right about and left her.

Then, when she went in to see her father and mother, there was such joy, there was no end to it. None of them thought they could thank her enough for all she had done for them. Now, they had everything they wished, as good as good could be, and they all wanted to know how she got on where she lived.

Well, she said, it was very good to live where she did; she had all she wished. What she said beside I don't know, but I don't think any of them had the right end of the stick, or that they got much out of her. But so, in the afternoon, after they had done dinner, all happened as the *White Bear* had said. Her mother wanted to talk with her alone in her bedroom; but she minded what the *White Bear* had said, and wouldn't go upstairs.

"Oh! what we have to talk about will keep!" she said, and put her mother off. But, somehow or other, her mother got round her at last, and she had to tell her the whole story. So she said, how every night when she had gone to bed a man came and lay down beside her as soon as she had put out the light; and how she never saw him, because he was always up and away before the morning dawned; and how she went about woeful and sorrowing, for she thought she should so like to see him; and how all day long she walked about there alone; and how dull and dreary and lonesome it was.

"My!" said her mother; "it may well be a Troll you slept with! But now I'll teach you a lesson how to set eyes on him. I'll give you a bit of candle, which you can carry home in your bosom; just light that while he is asleep, but take care not to drop the tallow on him."

Yes! she took the candle and hid it in her bosom, and as night drew on, the *White Bear* came and fetched her away.

But when they had gone a bit of the way, the *White Bear* asked if all hadn't happened as he had said.

"Well, she couldn't say it hadn't."

"Now, mind," said he, "if you have listened to your mother's advice, you have brought bad luck on us both, and then, all that has passed between us will be as nothing."

"No," she said, "she hadn't listened to her mother's advice."

So when she reached home, and had gone to bed, it was the old story over again. There came a man and lay down beside her; but at dead of night, when she heard he slept, she got up and struck a light, lit the candle, and let the light shine on him, and so she saw that he was the loveliest *Prince* one ever set eyes on, and she fell so deep in love with him on the spot, that she thought she couldn't live if she didn't give him a kiss there and then. And so she did; but as she kissed him, she dropped three hot drops of tallow on his shirt, and he woke up.

"What have you done?" he cried; "now you have made us both unlucky, for had you held out only this one year, I had been freed. For I have a step-mother who has bewitched me, so that I am a *White Bear* by day, and a *Man* by night. But now all ties are snapt between us; now I must set off from you to her. She lives in a Castle which stands *East of the Sun and West of the Moon*, and there, too, is a *Princess*, with a nose three ells long, and she's the wife I must have now."

She wept and took it ill, but there was no help for it; go he must.

Then she asked if she mightn't go with him.

No, she mightn't.

"Tell me the way, then," she said, "and I'll search you out; *that* surely I may get leave to do."

"Yes," she might do that, he said; "but there was no way to that place. It lay *East of the Sun and West of the Moon*, and thither she'd never find her way."

So next morning, when she woke up, both *Prince* and castle were gone, and then she lay on a little green patch, in the midst of the gloomy thick wood, and by her side lay the same bundle of rags she had brought with her from her old home.

So when she had rubbed the sleep out of her eyes, and wept till she was tired, she set out on her way, and walked many, many days, till she came to a lofty crag. Under it sat an old hag, and played with a gold apple which she tossed about. Her the lassie asked if she knew the way

"Tell me the way, then," she said, "and I'll search you out." Page 16

to the Prince, who lived with his step-mother in the Castle, that lay *East of the Sun and West of the Moon*, and who was to marry the *Princess* with a nose three ells long.

"How did you come to know about him?" asked the old hag; "but maybe you are the lassie who ought to have had him?"

Yes, she was.

"So, so; it's you, is it?" said the old hag. "Well, all I know about him is, that he lives in the castle that lies *East of the Sun and West of the Moon*, and thither you'll come, late or never; but still you may have the loan of my horse, and on him you can ride to my next neighbour. Maybe she'll be able to tell you; and when you get there, just give the horse a switch under the left ear, and beg him to be off home; and, stay, this gold apple you may take with you."

So she got upon the horse, and rode a long, long time, till she came to another crag, under which sat another old hag, with a gold carding-comb. Her the lassie asked if she knew the way to the castle that lay *East of the Sun and West of the Moon*, and she answered, like the first old hag, that she knew nothing about it, except it was east of the sun and west of the moon.

"And thither you'll come, late or never, but you shall have the loan of my horse to my next neighbour; maybe she'll tell you all about it; and when you get there, just switch the horse under the left ear, and beg him to be off home."

And this old hag gave her the golden carding-comb; it might be she'd find some use for it, she said. So the lassie got up on the horse, and rode a far, far way, and a weary time; and so at last she came to another great crag, under which sat another old hag, spinning with a golden spinning-wheel. Her, too, she asked if she knew the way to the *Prince*, and where the castle was that lay *East of the Sun and West of the Moon*. So it was the same thing over again.

"Maybe it's you who ought to have had the *Prince?*" said the old hag.

Yes, it was.

But she, too, didn't know the way a bit better than the other two. "East of the sun and west of the moon it was," she knew—that was all.

"And thither you'll come, late or never; but I'll lend you my horse, and then I think you'd best ride to the East Wind and ask him; maybe he knows those parts, and can blow you thither. But when you get to him, you need only give the horse a switch under the left ear, and he'll trot home of himself."

And so, too, she gave her the gold spinning-wheel. "Maybe you'll find a use for it," said the old hag.

Then on she rode many many days, a weary time, before she got to the East Wind's house, but at last she did reach it, and then she asked the East Wind if he could tell her the way to the *Prince* who dwelt east of the sun and west of the moon. Yes, the East Wind had often heard tell of it, the *Prince* and the castle, but he couldn't tell the way, for he had never blown so far.

"But, if you will, I'll go with you to my brother the West Wind, maybe he knows, for he's much stronger.

So, if you will just get on my back, I'll carry you thither."

Yes, she got on his back, and I should just think they went briskly along.

So when they got there, they went into the West Wind's house, and the East Wind said the lassie he had brought was the one who ought to have had the *Prince* who lived in the castle *East of the Sun and West of the Moon;* and so she had set out to seek him, and how he had come with her, and would be glad to know if the West Wind knew how to get to the castle.

"Nay," said the West Wind, "so far I've never blown; but if you will, I'll go with you to our brother the South Wind, for he's much stronger than either of us, and he has flapped his wings far and wide. Maybe he'll tell you. You can get on my back, and I'll carry you to him."

Yes! she got on his back, and so they travelled to the South Wind, and weren't so very long on the way, I should think.

When they got there, the West Wind asked him if he could tell her the way to the castle that lay *East of the Sun and West of the Moon*, for it was she who ought to have had the *Prince* who lived there.

"You don't say so! That's she, is it?" said the South Wind.

"Well, I have blustered about in most places in my time, but so far have I never blown; but if you will, I'll take you to my brother the North Wind; he is the oldest and strongest of the whole lot of us, and if he don't know where it is, you'll never find any one in the world to tell you. You can get on my back, and I'll carry you thither."

Yes! she got on his back, and away he went from his house at a fine rate. And this time, too, she wasn't long on her way.

So when they got to the North Wind's house, he was so wild and cross, cold puffs came from him a long way off.

"BLAST YOU BOTH, WHAT DO YOU WANT?" he roared out to them ever so far off, so that it struck them with an icy shiver.

"Well," said the South Wind, "you needn't be so foul-mouthed, for here I am, your brother, the South Wind, and here is the lassie who ought to have had the *Prince* who dwells in the castle that lies *East of the Sun and West of the Moon*, and now she wants to ask you if you ever were there, and can tell her the way, for she would be so glad to find him again."

"YES, I KNOW WELL ENOUGH WHERE IT IS," said the North

Wind; "once in my life I blew an aspen-leaf thither, but I was so tired I couldn't blow a puff for ever so many days after. But if you really wish to go thither, and aren't afraid to come along with me, I'll take you on my back and see if I can blow you thither."

Yes! with all her heart; she must and would get thither if it were possible in any way; and as for fear, however madly he went, she wouldn't be at all afraid.

"Very well, then," said the North Wind, "but you must sleep here to-night, for we must have the whole day before us, if we're to get thither at all."

Early next morning the North Wind woke her, and puffed himself up, and blew himself out, and made himself so stout and big, 'twas gruesome to look at him; and so off they went high up through the air, as if they would never stop till they got to the world's end.

Down here below there was such a storm; it threw down long tracts of wood and many houses, and when it swept over the great sea, ships foundered by hundreds.

So they tore on and on—no one can believe how far they went—and all the while they still went over the sea, and the North Wind got more and more weary, and so out of breath he could scarce bring out a puff, and his wings drooped and drooped, till at last he sunk so low that the crests of the waves dashed over his heels.

"Are you afraid?" said the North Wind.

"No!" she wasn't.

But they weren't very far from land; and the North Wind had still so much strength left in him that he managed to throw her up on the shore under the windows of the castle which lay *East of the Sun and West of the Moon;* but then he was so weak and worn out, he had to stay there and rest many days before he could get home again.

Next morning the lassie sat down under the castle window, and began to play with the gold apple; and the first person she saw was the *Long-nose* who was to have the *Prince*.

"What do you want for your gold apple, you lassie?" said the *Long-nose*, and threw up the window.

"It's not for sale, for gold or money," said the lassie.

"If it's not for sale for gold or money, what is it that you will sell it for? You may name your own price," said the *Princess*.

"Well! if I may get to the *Prince*, who lives here, and be with him to-night, you shall have it," said the lassie whom the North Wind had brought.

Yes! she might; that could be done. So the *Princess* got the gold apple; but when the lassie came up to the *Prince's* bed-room at night he was fast asleep; she called him and shook him, and between whiles she wept sore; but all she could do she couldn't wake him up. Next morning, as soon as day broke, came the *Princess* with the long nose, and drove her out again.

So in the daytime she sat down under the castle windows and began to card with her carding-comb, and the same thing happened. The *Princess* asked what she wanted for it; and she said it wasn't for sale for gold or money, but if she might get leave to go up to the *Prince* and be with him that night, the *Princess* should have it. But when she went up she found him fast asleep again, and all she called, and all she shook, and wept, and prayed, she couldn't get life into him; and as soon as the first gray peep of day came, then came the *Princess* with the long nose, and chased her out again.

So, in the daytime, the lassie sat down outside under the castle window, and began to spin with her golden spinning-wheel, and that, too, the *Princess* with the long nose wanted to have. So she threw up the window and asked what she wanted for it. The lassie said, as she had

And then she lay on a little green patch in the midst of the gloomy thick wood. Page 16

said twice before, it wasn't for sale for gold or money; but if she might go up to the *Prince* who was there, and be with him alone that night, she might have it.

Yes! she might do that and welcome. But now you must know there were some Christian folk who had been carried off thither, and as they sat in their room, which was next the *Prince*, they had heard how a woman had been in there, and wept and prayed, and called to him two nights running, and they told that to the *Prince*.

That evening, when the *Princess* came with her sleepy drink, the *Prince* made as if he drank, but threw it over over his shoulder, for he could guess it was a sleepy drink. So, when the lassie came in, she found the *Prince* wide awake; and then she told him the whole story how she had come thither.

"Ah," said the *Prince*, "you've just come in the very nick of time, for to-morrow is to be our wedding-day; but now I won't have the *Long-nose*, and you are the only woman in the world who can set me free. I'll say I want to see what my wife is fit for, and beg her to wash the shirt which has the three spots of tallow on it; she'll say yes, for she doesn't know 'tis you who put them there; but that's a work only for Christian folk, and not for such a pack of Trolls, and so I'll say that I won't have any other for my bride than the woman who can wash them out, and ask you to do it."

So there was great joy and love between them all that night. But next day, when the wedding was to be, the *Prince* said:

"First of all, I'd like to see what my bride is fit for."

"Yes!" said the step-mother, with all her heart.

"Well," said the *Prince*, "I've got a fine shirt which I'd like for my wedding shirt, but somehow or other it has got three spots of tallow on it, which I must have washed out; and I have sworn never to take any other bride than the woman who's able to do that. If she can't, she's not worth having."

Well, that was no great thing they said, so they agreed, and she with the long-nose began to wash away as hard as she could, but the more she rubbed and scrubbed, the bigger the spots grew.

"Ah!" said the old hag, her mother, "you can't wash; let me try."

But she hadn't long taken the shirt in hand before it got far worse than ever, and with all her rubbing, and wringing, and scrubbing, the spots grew bigger and blacker, and the darker and uglier was the shirt.

Then all the other Trolls began to wash, but the longer it lasted, the blacker and uglier the shirt grew, till at last it was as black all over as if it had been up the chimney.

"Ah!" said the *Prince*, "you're none of you worth a straw; you can't wash. Why there, outside, sits a beggar lassie, I'll be bound she knows how to wash better than the whole lot of you. COME IN, LASSIE!" he shouted.

Well, in she came.

"Can you wash this shirt clean, lassie you?" said he.

"I don't know," she said, "but I think I can."

And almost before she had taken it and dipped it in the water, it was as white as driven snow, and whiter still.

"Yes; you are the lassie for me," said the *Prince*.

At that the old hag flew into such a rage, she burst on the spot, and the *Princess* with the long nose after her, and the whole pack of Trolls after her—at least I've never heard a word about them since.

As for the *Prince* and *Princess*, they set free all the poor Christian folk who had been carried off and shut up there; and they took with them all the silver and gold, and flitted away as far as they could from the Castle that lay *East of the Sun and West of the Moon.*

THE BLUE BELT

ONCE on a time there was an old beggar-woman, who had gone out to beg. She had a little lad with her, and when she had got her bag full she struck across the hills towards her own home. So when they had gone a bit up the hill-side, they came upon a little *Blue Belt* which lay where two paths met, and the lad asked his mother's leave to pick it up.

"No," said she, "maybe there's witchcraft in it;" and so with threats she forced him to follow her. But when they had gone a bit further, the lad said he must turn aside a moment out of the road; and meanwhile his mother sat down on a tree-stump. But the lad was a long time gone, for as soon as he got so far into the wood that the old dame could not see him, he ran off to where the *Belt* lay, took it up, tied it round his waist, and lo! he felt as strong as if he could lift the whole hill. When he got back, the old dame was in a great rage, and wanted to know what he had been doing all that while. "You don't care how much time you waste, and yet you know the night is drawing on, and we must cross the hill before it is dark!" So on they tramped; but when they had got about half-way, the old dame grew weary, and said she must rest under a bush.

"Dear mother," said the lad, "mayn't I just go up to the top of this high crag while you rest, and try if I can't see some sign of folk hereabouts?"

Yes! he might do that; so when he had got to the top he saw a light shining from the north. So he ran down and told his mother.

"We must get on, mother; we are near a house, for I see a bright light shining quite close to us in the north." Then she rose and shouldered her bag, and set off to see; but they hadn't gone far, before there stood a steep spur of the hill, right across their path.

"Just as I thought!" said the old dame, "now we can't go a step farther; a pretty bed we shall have here!"

But the lad took the bag under one arm, and his mother under the other, and ran straight up the steep crag with them.

"Now, don't you see? Don't you see that we are close to a house? Don't you see that bright light?"

But the old dame said those were no Christian folk, but *Trolls*, for she was at home in all that forest far and near, and knew there was not a living soul in it, until you were well over the ridge and had come down on the other side. But they went on, and in a little while they came to a great house which was all painted red.

"What's the good?" said the old dame. "We daren't go in, for here the *Trolls* live."

"Don't say so; we must go in. There must be men where the lights shine so," said the lad. So in he went, and his mother after him, but he had scarce opened the door before she swooned away, for there she saw a great stout man, at least twenty feet high, sitting on the bench.

"Good evening, grandfather!" said the lad.

"Well, here I've sat three hundred years," said the man who sat on the bench, "and no one has ever come and called me grandfather before." Then the lad sat down by the man's side, and began to talk to him as if they had been old friends.

"But what's come over your mother?" said the man, after they had chatted a while. "I think she swooned away; you had better look after her."

So the lad went and took hold of the old dame, and dragged her up the hall along the floor. That brought her to herself, and she kicked and scratched, and flung herself about, and at last sat down upon a heap of firewood in the corner; but she was so frightened that she scarce dared to look one in the face.

After a while, the lad asked if they could spend the night there.

"Yes, to be sure," said the man.

So they went on talking again, but the lad soon got hungry, and wanted to know if they could get food as well as lodging.

"Of course," said the man, "that might be got too." And after he had sat a while longer, he rose up and threw six loads of dry pitch-pine on the fire. This made the old hag still more afraid.

"Oh! now he's going to roast us alive," she said, in the corner where she sat.

And when the wood had burned down to glowing embers, up got the man and strode out of his house.

"Heaven bless and help us! what a stout heart you have got!" said the old dame. "Don't you see we have got amongst *Trolls?*"

"Stuff and nonsense!" said the lad; "no harm if we have."

In a little while, back came the man with an ox so fat and big, the lad had never seen its like, and he gave it

The North Wind goes over the sea. Page 22

one blow with his fist under the ear, and down it fell dead on the floor. When that was done, he took it up by all the four legs and laid it on the glowing embers, and turned it and twisted it about till it was burnt brown outside. After that, he went to a cupboard and took out a great silver dish, and laid the ox on it; and the dish was so big that none of the ox hung over on any side. This he put on the table, and then he went down into the cellar and fetched a cask of wine, knocked out the head, and put the cask on the table, together with two knives, which were each six feet long. When this was done he bade them go and sit down to supper and eat. So they went, the lad first and the old dame after, but she began to whimper and wail, and to wonder how she should ever use such knives. But her son seized one, and began to cut slices out of the thigh of the ox, which he placed before his mother. And when they had eaten a bit, he took up the cask with both hands, and lifted it down to the floor; then he told his mother to come and drink, but it was still so high she couldn't reach up to it; so he caught her up, and held her up to the edge of the cask while she drank; as for himself, he clambered up and hung down like a cat inside the cask while he drank. So when he had quenched his thirst, he took up the cask and put it back on the table, and thanked the man for the good meal, and told his mother to come and thank him too, and, a-feared though she was, she dared do nothing else but thank the man. Then the lad sat down again alongside the man and began to gossip, and after they had sat a while the man said:

"Well! I must just go and get a bit of supper too;" and so he went to the table and ate up the whole ox—hoofs, and horns, and all—and drained the cask to the last drop, and then went back and sat on the bench.

"As for beds," he said, "I don't know what's to be done. I've only got one bed and a cradle; but we could get on pretty well if you would sleep in the cradle, and then your mother might lie in the bed yonder."

"Thank you kindly, that'll do nicely," said the lad; and with that he pulled off his clothes and lay down in the cradle; but, to tell you the truth, it was quite as big as a four-poster. As for the old dame, she had to follow the man who showed her to bed, though she was out of her wits for fear.

"Well!" thought the lad to himself, "'twill never do to go to sleep yet. I'd best lie awake and listen how things go as the night wears on."

So, after a while, the man began to talk to the old dame, and at last he said:

"We two might live here so happily together, could we only be rid of this son of yours."

"But do you know how to settle him? Is that what you're thinking of?" said she.

"Nothing easier," said he; at any rate he would try. He would just say he wished the old dame would stay and keep house for him a day or two, and then he would take the lad out with him up the hill to quarry corner-stones, and roll down a great rock on him. All this the lad lay and listened to.

Next day the *Troll*—for it was a *Troll* as clear as day—asked if the old dame would stay and keep house for him a few days; and as the day went on he took a great iron crowbar, and asked the lad if he had a mind to go with him up the hill and quarry a few corner-stones. With all his heart, he said, and went with him; and so, after they had split a few stones, the *Troll* wanted him to go down below and look after cracks in the rock; and while he was doing this the *Troll* worked away, and wearied himself with his crowbar till he moved a whole crag out of its bed, which came rolling right down on the place where the lad was; but he held it up till he could get on one side, and then let it roll on.

"Oh!" said the lad to the *Troll*, "now I see what you mean to do with me. You want to crush me to death; so just go down yourself and look after the cracks and refts in the rock, and I'll stand up above."

The *Troll* did not dare to do otherwise than the lad bade him, and the end of it was that the lad rolled down a great rock, which fell upon the *Troll* and broke one of his thighs.

"Well! you *are* in a sad plight," said the lad, as he strode down, lifted up the rock, and set the man free. After that he had to put him on his back and carry him home; so he ran with him as fast as a horse, and shook him so that the *Troll* screamed and screeched as if a knife were run into him. And when he got home, they had to put the *Troll* to bed, and there he lay in a sad pickle.

When the night wore on, the *Troll* began to talk to the old dame again, and to wonder how ever they could be rid of the lad.

"Well," said the old dame, "if you can't hit on a plan to get rid of him, I'm sure I can't."

"Let me see," said the *Troll;* "I've got twelve lions in a garden; if they could only get hold of the lad, they'd soon tear him to pieces."

So the old dame said it would be easy enough to get him there. She would sham sick, and say she felt so poorly, nothing would do her any good but lion's milk. All that the lad lay and listened to; and when he got up in the morning his mother said she was worse than she looked, and she thought she should never be right again unless she could get some lion's milk.

"Then I'm afraid you'll be poorly a long time, mother," said the lad, "for I'm sure I don't know where any is to be got."

"Oh! if that be all," said the *Troll,* "there's no lack of lion's milk, if we only had the man to fetch it;" and then he went on to say how his brother had a garden with twelve lions in it, and how the lad might have the key if he had a mind to milk the lions. So the lad took the key and a milking pail, and strode off; and when he unlocked the gate and got into the garden, there stood all the twelve lions on their hind-paws, rampant and roaring at him. But the lad laid hold of the biggest, and led him about by the fore-paws, and dashed him against stocks and stones till there wasn't a bit of him left but the two paws. So when the rest saw that, they were so afraid that they crept up and lay at his feet like so many curs. After that they followed him about wherever he went, and when he got home, they lay down outside the house, with their fore-paws on the door sill.

"Now, mother, you'll soon be well," said the lad, when he went in, "for here is the lion's milk."

He had just milked a drop in the pail.

But the Troll, as he lay in bed, swore it was all a lie. He was sure the lad was not the man to milk lions.

When the lad heard that, he forced the *Troll* to get out of bed, threw open the door, and all the lions rose up and seized the *Troll*, and at last the lad had to make them leave their hold.

That night the *Troll* began to talk to the old dame again. "I'm sure I can't tell how to put this lad out of the way—he is so awfully strong; can't you think of some way?"

"No," said the old dame, "if you can't tell, I'm sure I can't."

"Well!" said the *Troll*, "I have two brothers in a castle; they are twelve times as strong as I am, and that's why I was turned out and had to put up with this farm. They hold that castle, and round it there is an orchard with apples in it, and whoever eats those apples sleeps for three days and three nights. If we could only get the lad to go for the fruit, he wouldn't be able to keep from tasting the apples, and as soon as ever he fell asleep my brothers would tear him in pieces."

The old dame said she would sham sick, and say she could never be herself again unless she tasted those apples; for she had set her heart on them.

All this the lad lay and listened to.

When the morning came the old dame was so poorly that she couldn't utter a word but groans and sighs. She was sure she should never be well again, unless she had some of those apples that grew in the orchard near the castle where the man's brothers lived; only she had no one to send for them.

Oh! the lad was ready to go that instant; but the eleven lions went with him. So when he came to the orchard, he climbed up into the apple tree and ate as many apples as he could, and he had scarce got down before he fell into a deep sleep; but the lions all lay round him in a ring. The third day came the *Troll's* brothers, but they did not come in man's shape. They came snorting like man-eating steeds, and wondered who it was that dared to be there, and said they would tear him to pieces, so small that there should not be a bit of him left. But up rose the lions and tore the *Trolls* into small pieces, so that the place looked as if a dung heap had been tossed about it; and when they had finished the *Trolls* they lay down again. The lad did not wake till late in the afternoon, and when he got on his knees and rubbed the sleep out of his eyes, he began to wonder what had been going on, when he saw the marks of hoofs. But when he went towards the castle, a maiden looked out of a window who had seen all that had happened, and she said:

"You may thank your stars you weren't in that tussle, else you must have lost your life."

"What! I lose my life! No fear of that, I think," said the lad.

So she begged him to come in, that she might talk with him, for she hadn't seen a Christian soul ever since she came there. But when she opened the door the lions wanted to go in too, but she got so frightened that she began to scream, and so the lad let them lie outside.

And flitted away as far as they could from the Castle that lay East of the Sun and West of the Moon. Page 27

Then the two talked and talked, and the lad asked how it came that she, who was so lovely, could put up with those ugly *Trolls*. She never wished it, she said; 'twas quite against her will. They had seized her by force, and she was the King of Arabia's daughter. So they talked on, and at last she asked him what he would do; whether she should go back home, or whether he would have her to wife. Of course he would have her, and she shouldn't go home.

After that they went round the castle, and at last they came to a great hall, where the *Trolls'* two great swords hung high up on the wall.

"I wonder if you are man enough to wield one of these," said the *Princess.*

"Who? I?" said the lad. "'Twould be a pretty thing if I couldn't wield one of these."

With that he put two or three chairs one a-top of the other, jumped up, and touched the biggest sword with his finger tips, tossed it up in the air, and caught it again by the hilt; leapt down, and at the same time dealt such a blow with it on the floor that the whole hall shook. After he had thus got down, he thrust the sword under his arm and carried it about with him.

So, when they had lived a little while in the castle, the *Princess* thought she ought to go home to her parents, and let them know what had become of her; so they loaded a ship, and she set sail from the castle.

After she had gone, and the lad had wandered about a little, he called to mind that he had been sent out on an errand thither, and had come to fetch something for his mother's health; and though he said to himself, "After all the old dame was not so bad but she's all right by this time"—still he thought he ought to go and just see how she was. So he went and found both the man and his mother quite fresh and hearty.

"What wretches you are to live in this beggarly hut," said the lad. "Come with me up to my castle, and you shall see what a fine fellow I am."

Well! they were both ready to go, and on the way his mother talked to him, and asked how it was he had got so strong.

"If you must know it came of that blue belt which lay on the hill-side that time when you and I were out begging," said the lad.

"Have you got it still?" asked she.

"Yes"—he had. It was tied round his waist.

"Might she see it?"

"Yes"—she might; and with that he pulled open his waistcoat and shirt to show it her.

Then she seized it with both hands, tore it off, and twisted it round her fist.

"Now," she cried, "what shall I do with such a wretch as you? I'll just give you one blow, and dash your brains out!"

"Far too good a death for such a scamp," said the *Troll*. "No! let's first burn out his eyes, and then turn him adrift in a little boat."

So they burned out his eyes and turned him adrift, in spite of his prayers and tears; but, as the boat drifted, the lions swam after, and at last they laid hold of it and dragged it ashore on an island, and placed the lad under a fir tree. They caught game for him, and they plucked the birds and made him a bed of down; but he was forced to eat his meat raw and he was blind. At last, one day the biggest lion was chasing a hare which was blind, for it ran straight over stock and stone, and the end was, it ran right up against a fir-stump and tumbled head over heels across the field right into a spring; but lo! when it came out of the spring it saw its way quite plain, and so saved its life.

"So, so!" thought the lion, and went and dragged the lad to the spring, and dipped him over head and ears in it. So, when he had got his sight again, he went down to the shore and made signs to the lions that they should all lie close together like a raft; then he stood upon their backs while they swam with him to the mainland. When he had reached the shore he went up into a birchen copse, and made the lions lie quiet. Then he stole up to the castle, like a thief, to see if he couldn't lay hands on his belt; and when he got to the door, he peeped through the keyhole, and there he saw his belt hanging up over a door in the kitchen. So he crept softly in across the floor, for there was no one there; but as soon as he had got hold of the belt, he began to kick and stamp about as though he were mad. Just then his mother came rushing out:

"Dear heart, my darling little boy! do give me the belt again," she said.

"Thank you kindly," said he. "Now you shall have the doom you passed on me," and he fulfilled it on the spot. When the old *Troll* heard that, he came in and begged and prayed so prettily that he might not be smitten to death.

"Well, you may live," said the lad, "but you shall undergo the same punishment you gave me;" and so he burned out the *Troll's* eyes, and turned him adrift on the sea in a little boat, but he had no lions to follow him.

Now the lad was all alone, and he went about longing and longing for the *Princess*; at last he could bear it no longer; he must set out to seek her, his heart was so bent on having her. So he loaded four ships and set sail for Arabia.

For some time they had fair wind and fine weather, but after that they lay wind-bound under a rocky island. So the sailors went ashore and strolled about to spend the time, and there they found a huge egg, almost as big as a little house. So they began to knock it about with large stones, but, after all, they couldn't crack the shell. Then the lad came up with his sword to see what all the noise was about, and when he saw the egg, he thought it a trifle to crack it; so he gave it one blow and the egg split, and out came a chicken as big as an elephant.

"Now we have done wrong," said the lad; "this can cost us all our lives;" and then he asked his sailors if they were men enough to sail to Arabia in four-and-twenty hours if they got a fine breeze. Yes! they were good to do that, they said, so they set sail with a fine breeze, and got to Arabia in three-and-twenty hours. As soon as they landed, the lad ordered all the sailors to go and bury themselves up to the eyes in a sandhill, so that they could barely see the ships. The lad and the captains climbed a high crag and sate down under a fir.

In a little while came a great bird flying with an island in its claws, and let it fall down on the fleet, and sunk every ship. After it had done that, it flew up to the sandhill and flapped its wings, so that the wind nearly took off the heads of the sailors, and it flew past the fir with such force that it turned the lad right about, but he was ready with his sword, and gave the bird one blow and brought it down dead.

After that he went to the town, where every one was glad because the *King* had got his daughter back; but now the *King* had hidden her away somewhere himself, and promised her hand as a reward to any one who could find her, and this though she was betrothed before. Now as the lad went along he met a man who had white bear-skins for sale, so he bought one of the hides and put it on; and one of the captains was to take an iron chain and lead him about, and so he went into the town and began to play pranks. At last the news came to the *King's* ears, that there never had been such fun in the town before, for here was a white bear that danced and cut capers just as it was bid. So a messenger came to say the bear must come to the castle at once, for the *King* wanted to see its tricks. So when it got to the castle every one was afraid, for such a beast they had never seen before; but the captain said there was no danger unless they laughed at it. They mustn't do that, else it would tear them to pieces. When the *King* heard that, he warned all the court not to laugh. But while the fun was going on, in came one of the *King's* maids, and began to laugh and make game of the bear, and the bear flew at her and tore her, so that there was scarce a rag of her left. Then all the court began to bewail, and the captain most of all.

"Stuff and nonsense," said the *King*; "she's only a maid, besides it's more my affair than yours."

When the show was over, it was late at night. "It's no good your going away, when it's so late," said the *King*. "The bear had best sleep here."

"Perhaps it might sleep in the ingle by the kitchen fire," said the captain.

"Nay," said the *King*, "it shall sleep up here, and it shall have pillows and cushions to sleep on." So a whole heap of pillows and cushions was brought, and the captain had a bed in a side room.

But at midnight the *King* came with a lamp in his hand

and a big bunch of keys, and carried off the white bear. He passed along gallery after gallery, through doors and rooms, up-stairs and down-stairs, till at last he came to a pier which ran out into the sea. Then the *King* began to pull and haul at posts and pins, this one up and that one down, till at last a little house floated up to the water's edge. There he kept his daughter, for she was so dear to him that he had hid her, so that no one could find her out. He left the white bear outside while he went in and told her how it had danced and played its pranks. She said she was afraid, and dared not look at it; but he talked her over, saying there was no danger if she only wouldn't laugh. So they brought the bear in, and locked the door, and it danced and played

The Lad in the Bear's skin, and the King of Arabia's daughter. *Page* 49

its tricks; but just when the fun was at its height, the *Princess's* maid began to laugh. Then the lad flew at her and tore her to bits, and the *Princess* began to cry and sob.

"Stuff and nonsense," cried the *King*; "all this fuss about a maid! I'll get you just as good a one again. But now I think the bear had best stay here till morning, for I don't care to have to go and lead it along all those galleries and stairs at this time of night."

"Well!" said the *Princess*, "if it sleeps here, I'm sure I won't."

But just then the bear curled himself up and lay down by the stove; and it was settled at last that the *Princess* should sleep there too, with a light burning. But as soon as the *King* had well gone, the white bear came and begged her to undo his collar. The *Princess* was so scared she almost swooned away; but she felt about till she found the collar, and she had scarce undone it before the bear pulled his head off. Then she knew him again, and was so glad there was no end to her joy, and she wanted to tell her father at once that her deliverer was come. But the lad would not hear of it; he would earn her once more, he said. So in the morning when they heard the *King* rattling at the posts outside, the lad drew on the hide and lay down by the stove.

"Well, has it lain still?" the king asked.

"I should think so," said the *Princess*; "it hasn't so much as turned or stretched itself once."

When they got up to the castle again, the captain took the bear and led it away, and then the lad threw off the hide, and went to a tailor and ordered clothes fit for a prince; and when they were fitted on he went to the *King*, and said he wanted to find the *Princess*.

"You're not the first who has wished the same thing," said the *King*, "but they have all lost their lives; for if any one who tries can't find her in four-and-twenty hours his life is forfeited."

Yes; the lad knew all that. Still he wished to try,

and if he couldn't find her, 'twas his look-out. Now in the castle there was a band that played sweet tunes, and there were fair maids to dance with, and so the lad danced away.

When twelve hours were gone, the *King* said:

"I pity you with all my heart. You're so poor a hand at seeking; you will surely lose your life."

"Stuff!" said the lad; "while there's life there's hope! So long as there's breath in the body there's no fear; we have lots of time!" and so he went on dancing till there was only one hour left.

Then he said he would begin to search.

"It's no use now," said the *King*; "time's up."

"Light your lamp; out with your big bunch of keys," said the lad, "and follow me whither I wish to go. There is still a whole hour left."

So the lad went the same way which the *King* had led him the night before, and he bade the *King* unlock door after door till they came down to the pier which ran out into the sea.

"It's all no use, I tell you," said the *King*; "time's up, and this will only lead you right out into the sea."

"Still five minutes more," said the lad, as he pulled and pushed at the posts and pins, and the house floated up.

"Now the time is up," bawled the *King*; "come hither, headsman, and take off his head."

"Nay, nay!" said the lad; "stop a bit, there are still three minutes! Out with the key, and let me get into this house."

But there stood the *King* and fumbled with his keys, to draw out the time. At last he said he hadn't any key.

"Well, if you haven't, I *have*," said the lad, as he gave the door such a kick that it flew to splinters inwards on the floor.

At the door the *Princess* met him, and told her father this was her deliverer, on whom her heart was set. So she had him; and this was how the beggar boy came to marry the daughter of the King of Arabia.

PRINCE LINDWORM

ONCE upon a time, there was a fine young *King* who was married to the loveliest of Queens. They were exceedingly happy, all but for one thing—they had no children. And this often made them both sad, because the *Queen* wanted a dear little child to play with, and the *King* wanted an heir to the kingdom.

One day the *Queen* went out for a walk by herself, and she met an ugly old woman. The old woman was just like a witch: but she was a nice kind of witch, not the cantankerous sort. She said, "Why do you look so doleful, pretty lady?" "It's no use my telling you," answered the *Queen*, "nobody in the world can help me." "Oh, you never know," said the old woman. "Just you let me hear what your trouble is, and maybe I can put things right."

"My dear woman, how can you?" said the *Queen*: and she told her, "The *King* and I have no children: that's why I am so distressed." "Well, you needn't be," said the old witch. "I can set that right in a twinkling, if only you will do exactly as I tell you. Listen. To-night, at sunset, take a little drinking-cup with two ears" (that is, handles), "and put it bottom upwards on the ground in the north-west corner of your garden. Then go and lift it up to-morrow morning at sunrise, and you will find two roses underneath it, one red and one white. If you eat the red rose, a little boy will be born to you: if you eat the white rose, a little girl will be sent. But, whatever you do, you mustn't eat *both* the roses, or you'll be sorry,—that I warn you! Only one: remember that!" "Thank you a thousand times," said the *Queen*, "this is good news indeed!" And she wanted to give the old woman her gold ring; but the old woman wouldn't take it.

So the *Queen* went home and did as she had been told: and next morning at sunrise she stole out into the garden and lifted up the little drinking-cup. She *was* surprised, for indeed she had hardly expected to see anything. But there were the two roses underneath it, one red and one white. And now she was dreadfully puzzled, for she did not know which to choose. "If I choose the red one," she thought, "and I have a little boy, he may grow up and go to the wars and get killed. But if I choose the white one, and have a little girl, she will stay at home awhile with us, but later on she will get married and go away and leave us. So, whichever it is, we may be left with no child after all."

However, at last she decided on the white rose, and she ate it. And it tasted so sweet, that she took and ate the red one too: without ever remembering the old woman's solemn warning.

Some time after this, the King went away to the wars: and while he was still away, the *Queen* became the mother of twins. One was a lovely baby-boy, and the other was a *Lindworm*, or Serpent. She was terribly frightened when she saw the *Lindworm*, but he wriggled away out of the room, and nobody seemed to have seen him but herself: so that she thought it must have been a dream. The baby *Prince* was so beautiful and so healthy, the

Queen was full of joy: and likewise, as you may suppose, was the *King* when he came home and found his son and heir. Not a word was said by anyone about the *Lindworm*: only the *Queen* thought about it now and then.

Many days and years passed by, and the baby grew up into a handsome young *Prince*, and it was time that he got married. The *King* sent him off to visit foreign kingdoms, in the Royal coach, with six white horses, to look for a Princess grand enough to be his wife. But at the very first cross-roads, the way was stopped by an enormous *Lindworm*, enough to frighten the bravest. He lay in the middle of the road with a great wide open mouth, and cried, "A bride for me before a bride for you!" Then the *Prince* made the coach turn round and try another road: but it was all no use. For, at the first cross-ways, there lay the *Lindworm* again, crying out, "A bride for me before a bride for you!" So the *Prince* had to turn back home again to the Castle, and give up his visits to the foreign kingdoms. And his mother, the *Queen*, had to confess that what the *Lindworm* said was true. For he was really the eldest of her twins: and so he ought to have a wedding first.

There seemed nothing for it but to find a bride for the

She saw the Lindworm for the first time as he came in and stood by her side. *Page* 61

Lindworm, if his younger brother, the *Prince*, were to be married at all. So the *King* wrote to a distant country, and asked for a Princess to marry his son (but, of course, he didn't say which son), and presently a Princess arrived. But she wasn't allowed to see her bridegroom until he stood by her side in the great hall and was married to her, and then, of course, it was too late for her to say she wouldn't have him. But next morning the Princess had disappeared. The *Lindworm* lay sleeping all alone: and it was quite plain that he had eaten her.

A little while after, the *Prince* decided that he might now go journeying again in search of a *Princess*. And off he drove in the Royal chariot with the six white horses. But at the first cross-ways, there lay the *Lindworm*, crying with his great wide open mouth, "A bride for me before a bride for you!" So the carriage tried another road, and the same thing happened, and they had to turn back again this time, just as formerly. And the *King* wrote to several foreign countries, to know if anyone would marry his son. At last another *Princess* arrived, this time from a very far distant land. And, of course, she was not allowed to see her future husband before the wedding took place,—and then, lo and behold! it was the *Lindworm* who stood at her side. And next morning the Princess had disappeared: and the *Lindworm* lay sleeping all alone; and it was quite clear that he had eaten her.

By and by the *Prince* started on his quest for the third time: and at the first cross-roads there lay the *Lindworm* with his great wide open mouth, demanding a bride as before. And the *Prince* went straight back to the castle, and told the *King*: "You must find another bride for my elder brother."

"I don't know where I am to find her," said the *King*, "I have already made enemies of two great Kings who sent their daughters here as brides: and I have no notion how I can obtain a third lady. People are beginning to say strange things, and I am sure no *Princess* will dare to come."

Now, down in a little cottage near a wood, there lived the *King's* shepherd, an old man with his only daughter. And the *King* came one day and said to him, "Will you give me your daughter to marry my son the *Lindworm?* And I will make you rich for the rest of your life."—"No, sire," said the shepherd, "that I cannot do. She is my only child, and I want her to take care of me when

I am old. Besides, if the *Lindworm* would not spare two beautiful Princesses, he won't spare her either. He will just gobble her up: and she is much too good for such a fate."

But the *King* wouldn't take "No" for an answer: and at last the old man had to give in.

Well, when the old shepherd told his daughter that she was to be *Prince Lindworm's* bride, she was utterly in despair. She went out into the woods, crying and wringing her hands and bewailing her hard fate. And while she wandered to and fro, an old witch-woman suddenly appeared out of a big hollow oak-tree, and asked her, "Why do you look so doleful, pretty lass?" The shepherd-girl said, "It's no use my telling you, for nobody in the world can help me."—"Oh, you never know," said the old woman. "Just you let me hear what your trouble is, and maybe I can put things right."—"Ah, how can you?" said the girl, "For I am to be married to the *King's* eldest son, who is a *Lindworm.* He has already married two beautiful Princesses, and devoured them: and he will eat me too! No wonder I am distressed."

"Well, you needn't be," said the witchwoman. "All

that can be set right in a twinkling: if only you will do exactly as I tell you." So the girl said she would.

"Listen, then," said the old woman. "After the marriage ceremony is over, and when it is time for you to retire to rest, you must ask to be dressed in ten snow-white shifts. And you must then ask for a tub full of lye," (that is, washing water prepared with wood-ashes) "and a tub full of fresh milk, and as many whips as a boy can carry in his arms,—and have all these brought into your bed-chamber. Then, when the *Lindworm* tells you to shed a shift, do you bid him slough a skin. And when all his skins are off, you must dip the whips in the lye and whip him; next, you must wash him in the fresh milk; and, lastly, you must take him and hold him in your arms, if it's only for one moment."

"The last is the worst notion—ugh!" said the shepherd's daughter, and she shuddered at the thought of holding the cold, slimy, scaly *Lindworm*.

"Do just as I have said, and all will go well," said the old woman. Then she disappeared again in the oak-tree.

When the wedding-day arrived, the girl was fetched in the Royal chariot with the six white horses, and taken to the castle to be decked as a bride. And she asked for ten snow-white shifts to be brought her, and the tub of lye, and the tub of milk, and as many whips as a boy could carry in his arms. The ladies and courtiers in the castle thought, of course, that this was some bit of peasant superstition, all rubbish and nonsense. But the *King* said, "Let her have whatever she asks for." She was then arrayed in the most wonderful robes, and looked the loveliest of brides. She was led to the hall where the wedding ceremony was to take place, and she saw the *Lindworm* for the first time as he came in and stood by her side. So they were married, and a great wedding-feast was held, a banquet fit for the son of a king.

When the feast was over, the bridegroom and bride were conducted to their apartment, with music, and torches, and a great procession. As soon as the door was shut, the *Lindworm* turned to her and said, "Fair maiden, shed a shift!" The shepherd's daughter answered him, "*Prince Lindworm*, slough a skin!"—"No one has ever dared tell me to do that before!" said he.—"But I command you to do it now!" said she. Then he began to moan and wriggle: and in a few minutes a long snake-skin lay upon the floor beside him.

The girl drew off her first shift, and spread it on top of the skin.

The *Lindworm* said again to her, "Fair maiden, shed a shift."

The shepherd's daughter answered him, "*Prince Lindworm*, slough a skin."

"No one has ever dared tell me to do that before," said he.—"But I command you to do it now," said she. Then with groans and moans he cast off the second skin: and she covered it with her second shift. The *Lindworm* said for the third time, "Fair maiden, shed a shift." The shepherd's daughter answered him again, "*Prince Lindworm*, slough a skin."—"No one has ever dared tell me to do that before," said he, and his little eyes rolled furiously. But the girl was not afraid, and once more she commanded him to do as she bade.

And so this went on until nine *Lindworm* skins were lying on the floor, each of them covered with a snow-white shift. And there was nothing left of the *Lindworm* but a huge thick mass, most horrible to see. Then the girl seized the whips, dipped them in the lye, and whipped him as hard as ever she could. Next, she bathed him all over in the fresh milk. Lastly, she dragged him on to the bed and put her arms round him. And she fell fast asleep that very moment.

Next morning very early, the *King* and the courtiers came and peeped in through the keyhole. They wanted to know what had become of the girl, but none of them dared enter the room. However, in the end, growing bolder, they opened the door a tiny bit. And there they saw the girl, all fresh and rosy, and beside her lay—no *Lindworm*, but the handsomest prince that any one could wish to see.

The *King* ran out and fetched the *Queen*: and after that, there were such rejoicings in the castle as never were known before or since. The wedding took place all over again, much finer than the first, with festivals and banquets and merrymakings for days and weeks. No bride was ever so beloved by a King and Queen as this peasant maid from the shepherd's cottage. There was no end to their love and their kindness towards her: because, by her sense and her calmness and her courage, she had saved their son, *Prince Lindworm.*

She could not help setting the door a little ajar, just to peep in, when—Pop! out flew the Moon. Page 67

THE LASSIE AND HER GODMOTHER

ONCE on a time a poor couple lived far, far away in a great wood. The wife was brought to bed, and had a pretty girl, but they were so poor they did not know how to get the babe christened, for they had no money to pay the parson's fees. So one day the father went out to see if he could find any one who was willing to stand for the child and pay the fees; but though he walked about the whole day from one house to another, and though all said they were willing enough to stand, no one thought himself bound to pay the fees. Now, when he was going home

again, a lovely lady met him, dressed so fine, and she looked so thoroughly good and kind; she offered to get the babe christened, but after that, she said, she must keep it for her own. The husband answered, he must first ask his wife what she wished to do; but when he got home and told his story, the wife said, right out, "No!"

Next day the man went out again, but no one would stand if they had to pay the fees; and though he begged and prayed, he could get no help. And again as he went home, towards evening the same lovely lady met him, who looked so sweet and good, and she made him the same offer. So he told his wife again how he had fared, and this time she said, if he couldn't get any one to stand for his babe next day, they must just let the lady have her way, since she seemed so kind and good.

The third day, the man went about, but he couldn't get any one to stand; and so when, towards evening, he met the kind lady again, he gave his word she should have the babe if she would only get it christened at the font. So next morning she came to the place where the man lived, followed by two men to stand godfathers, took the babe and carried it to church, and there it was christened. After that she took it to her own house, and there the little girl lived with her several years, and her *Foster-mother* was always kind and friendly to her.

Now, when the *Lassie* had grown to be big enough to know right and wrong, her *Foster-mother* got ready to go on a journey.

"You have my leave," she said, "to go all over the house, except those rooms which I shew you;" and when she had said that, away she went.

But the *Lassie* could not forbear just to open one of the doors a little bit, when—Pop! out flew a Star.

When her *Foster-mother* came back, she was very vexed to find that the star had flown out, and she got very angry with her *Foster-daughter*, and threatened to send her away; but the child cried and begged so hard that she got leave to stay.

Now, after a while, the *Foster-mother* had to go on another journey; and, before she went, she forbade the *Lassie* to go into those two rooms into which she had never been. She promised to beware; but when she was left alone, she began to think and to wonder what there could be in the second room, and at last she could not help setting the door a little ajar, just to peep in, when—Pop! out flew the Moon.

When her *Foster-mother* came home and found the moon let out, she was very downcast, and said to the *Lassie* she must go away, she could not stay with her any longer. But the *Lassie* wept so bitterly, and prayed so heartily for forgiveness, that this time, too, she got leave to stay.

Some time after, the *Foster-mother* had to go away again, and she charged the Lassie, who by this time was half grown up, most earnestly that she mustn't try to go into, or to peep into, the third room. But when her *Foster-mother* had been gone some time, and the *Lassie* was weary of walking about alone, all at once she thought, "Dear me, what fun it would be just to peep a little into that third room." Then she thought she mustn't do it for her *Foster-mother's* sake; but when the bad thought came the second time she could hold out no longer; come what might, she must and would look into the room; so she just opened the door a tiny bit, when—POP! out flew the Sun.

But when her *Foster-mother* came back and saw that the sun had flown away, she was cut to the heart, and said, "Now, there was no help for it, the *Lassie* must and should go away; she couldn't hear of her staying any longer." Now the *Lassie* cried her eyes out, and begged and prayed so prettily; but it was all no good.

"Nay! but I must punish you!" said her *Foster-mother*; "but you may have your choice, either to be the loveliest woman in the world, and not to be able to speak, or to keep your speech, and to be the ugliest of all women; but away from me you must go."

And the *Lassie* said, "I would sooner be lovely." So she became all at once wondrous fair; but from that day forth she was dumb.

So, when she went away from her *Foster-mother*, she walked and wandered through a great, great wood; but the farther she went, the farther off the end seemed to be.

So, when the evening came on, she clomb up into a tall tree, which grew over a spring, and there she made herself up to sleep that night. Close by lay a castle, and from that castle came early every morning a maid to draw water to make the Prince's tea, from the spring over which the *Lassie* was sitting. So the maid looked down into the spring, saw the lovely face in the water, and thought it was her own; then she flung away the pitcher, and ran home; and, when she got there, she tossed up her head and said, "If I'm so pretty, I'm far too good to go and fetch water."

So another maid had to go for the water, but the same thing happened to her; she went back and said she was far too pretty and too good to fetch water from the spring for the Prince. Then the Prince went himself, for he had a mind to see what all this could mean. So, when he reached the spring, he too saw the image in the water; but he looked up at once, and became aware of the lovely *Lassie* who sate there up in the tree. Then he coaxed her down and took her home; and at last made up his mind to have her for his queen, because she was so lovely; but his mother, who was still alive, was against it.

"She can't speak," she said, "and maybe she's a wicked witch."

But the Prince could not be content till he got her. So after they had lived together a while, the *Lassie* was to have a child, and when the child came to be born, the Prince set a strong watch about her; but at the birth one and all fell into a deep sleep, and her *Foster-mother* came, cut the babe on its little finger, and smeared the queen's mouth with the blood; and said:

"Now you shall be as grieved as I was when you let out the star;" and with these words she carried off the babe.

But when those who were on the watch woke, they thought the queen had eaten her own child, and the old queen was all for burning her alive, but the Prince was so fond of her that at last he begged her off, but he had hard work to set her free.

So the next time the young queen was to have a child, twice as strong a watch was set as the first time, but the same thing happened over again, only this time her *Foster-mother* said:

"Now you shall be as grieved as I was when you let the moon out."

And the queen begged and prayed, and wept; for when her *Foster-mother* was there, she could speak—but it was all no good.

And now the old queen said she must be burnt, but the Prince found means to beg her off. But when the third child was to be born, a watch was set three times as strong as the first, but just the same thing happened. Her *Foster-mother* came while the watch slept, took the babe, and cut its little finger, and smeared the queen's mouth with the blood, telling her now she should be as grieved as she had been when the *Lassie* let out the sun.

And now the Prince could not save her any longer. She must and should be burnt. But just as they were leading her to the stake, all at once they saw her *Foster-mother*, who came with all three children—two she led by the hand, and the third she had on her arm; and so she went up to the young queen and said:

"Here are your children; now you shall have them again. I am the Virgin Mary, and so grieved as you have been, so grieved was I when you let out sun, and moon, and star. Now you have been punished for what you did, and henceforth you shall have your speech."

Then he coaxed her down and took her home. *Page 70*

How glad the Queen and Prince now were, all may easily think, but no one can tell. After that they were always happy; and from that day even the Prince's mother was very fond of the young queen.

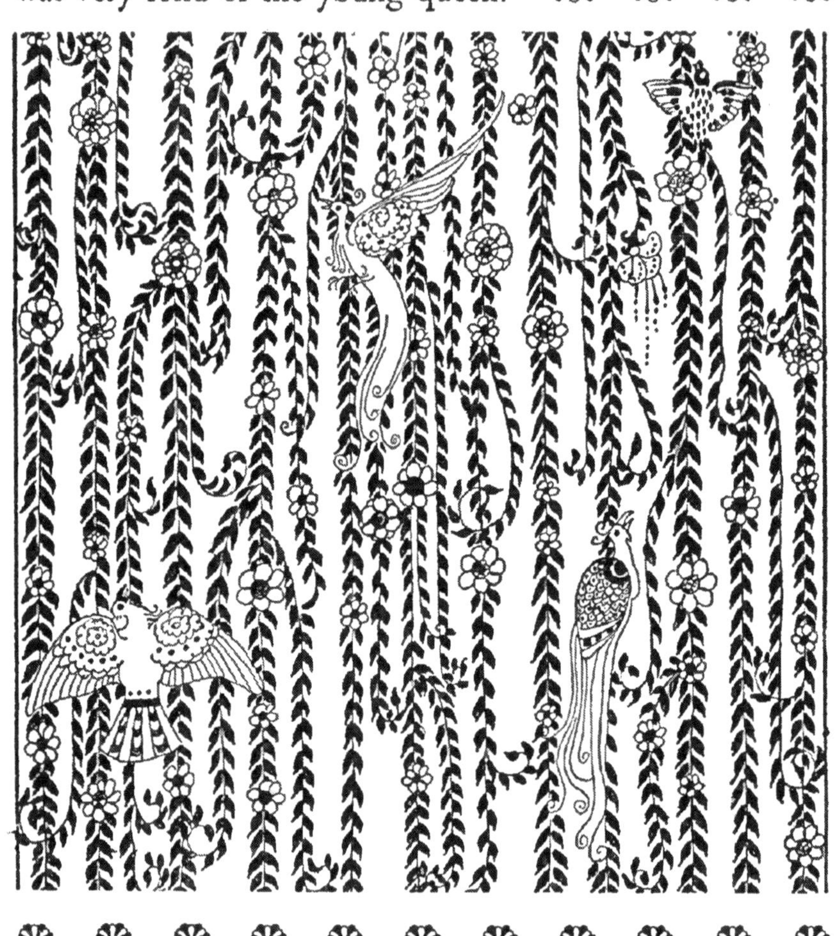

K.

THE HUSBAND WHO WAS TO MIND THE HOUSE

ONCE on a time there was a man, so surly and cross, he never thought his *Wife* did anything right in the house. So, one evening, in haymaking time, he came home, scolding and swearing, and showing his teeth and making a dust.

"Dear love, don't be so angry; there's a good man," said his goody; "to-morrow let's change our work. I'll go out with the mowers and mow, and you shall mind the house at home."

Yes! the *Husband* thought that would do very well. He was quite willing, he said.

So, early next morning, his goody took a scythe over her neck, and went out into the hayfield with the mowers, and began to mow; but the man was to mind the house, and do the work at home.

First of all, he wanted to churn the butter; but when he had churned a while, he got thirsty, and went down to the cellar to tap a barrel of ale. So, just when he had knocked in the bung, and was putting the tap into the cask, he heard overhead the pig come into the kitchen,

Then off he ran up the cellar steps, with the tap in his hand, as fast as he could, to look after the pig, lest it should upset the churn; but when he got up, and saw the pig had already knocked the churn over, and stood there, routing and grunting amongst the cream which was running all over the floor, he got so wild with rage that he quite forgot the ale-barrel, and ran at the pig as hard as he could. He caught it, too, just as it ran out of doors, and gave it such a kick, that piggy lay for dead on the spot. Then all at once he remembered he had the tap in his hand; but when he got down to the cellar, every drop of ale had run out of the cask.

Then he went into the dairy and found enough cream left to fill the churn again, and so he began to churn, for butter they must have at dinner. When he had churned a bit, he remembered that their milking cow was still shut up in the byre, and hadn't had a bit to eat or a drop to drink all the morning, though the sun was high. Then all at once he thought 'twas too far to take her down to the meadow, so he'd just get her up on the house top—for the house, you must know, was thatched with sods, and a fine crop of grass was growing there. Now the house lay close up against a steep down, and he thought if he laid a plank across to the thatch at the back he'd easily get the cow up.

But still he couldn't leave the churn, for there was his little babe crawling about on the floor, and "if I leave it," he thought, "the child is safe to upset it." So he took the churn on his back, and went out with it; but then he thought he'd better first water the cow before he turned her out on the thatch; so he took up a bucket to draw water out of the well; but, as he stooped down at the well's brink, all the cream ran out of the churn over his shoulders, and so down into the well.

Now it was near dinner-time, and he hadn't even got the butter yet; so he thought he'd best boil the porridge, and filled the pot with water and hung it over the fire. When he had done that, he thought the cow might perhaps fall off the thatch and break her legs or her neck. So he got up on the house to tie her up. One end of the rope he made fast to the cow's neck and the other he slipped down the chimney and tied round his own thigh; and he had to make haste, for the water now began to boil in the pot, and he had still to grind the oatmeal.

So he began to grind away; but while he was hard at it, down fell the cow off the house-top after all, and as she fell, she dragged the man up the chimney by the rope. There he stuck fast; and as for the cow, she hung half-way down the wall, swinging between heaven and earth, for she could neither get down nor up.

And now the goody had waited seven lengths and seven breadths for her *Husband* to come and call them home to dinner; but never a call they had. At last she thought she'd waited long enough, and went home. But when she got there and saw the cow hanging in such an ugly

place, she ran up and cut the rope in two with her scythe. But, as she did this, down came her *Husband* out of the chimney; and so, when his old dame came inside the kitchen, there she found him standing on his head in the porridge pot.

THE LAD WHO WENT TO THE NORTH WIND

ONCE on a time there was an old widow who had one son; and as she was poorly and weak, her son had to go up into the safe to fetch meal for cooking; "but when he got outside the safe, and was just going down the steps, there came the *North Wind* puffing and blowing, caught up the meal, and so away with it through the air. Then the *Lad* went back into the safe for more; but when he came out again on the steps, if the *North Wind* didn't come again and carry off the meal with a puff: and, more than that, he did so the third time. At this

the *Lad* got very angry; and as he thought it hard that the *North Wind* should behave so, he thought he'd just look him up, and ask him to give up his meal.

So off he went, but the way was long, and he walked and walked; but at last he came to the *North Wind's* house.

"Good day!" said the *Lad*, "and thank you for coming to see us yesterday."

"GOOD DAY!" answered the *North Wind*, for his voice was loud and gruff, "AND THANKS FOR COMING TO SEE ME. WHAT DO YOU WANT?"

"Oh!" answered the *Lad*, "I only wished to ask you to be so good as to let me have back that meal you took from me on the safe steps, for we haven't much to live on; and if you're to go on snapping up the morsel we have, there'll be nothing for it but to starve."

"I haven't got your meal," said the *North Wind*; "but if you are in such need, I'll give you a cloth which will get you everything you want, if you only say, 'Cloth, spread yourself, and serve up all kinds of good dishes!'"

With this the *Lad* was well content. But, as the way was so long he couldn't get home in one day, so he turned into an inn on the way; and when they were going

"Here are your children; now you shall have them again. I am the Virgin Mary." Page 72

to sit down to supper he laid the cloth on a table which stood in the corner, and said:

"Cloth, spread yourself, and serve up all kinds of good dishes."

He had scarce said so before the cloth did as it was bid; and all who stood by thought it a fine thing, but most of all the landlady. So, when all were fast asleep at dead of night, she took the *Lad's* cloth, and put another in its stead, just like the one he had got from the *North Wind*, but which couldn't so much as serve up a bit of dry bread.

So, when the *Lad* woke, he took his cloth and went off with it, and that day he got home to his mother.

"Now," said he, "I've been to the *North Wind's* house, and a good fellow he is, for he gave me this cloth, and when I only say to it, 'Cloth, spread yourself, and serve up all kinds of good dishes,' I get any sort of food I please."

"All very true, I daresay," said his mother; "but seeing is believing, and I shan't believe it till I see it."

So the *Lad* made haste, drew out a table, laid the cloth on it, and said:

"Cloth, spread yourself, and serve up all kinds of good dishes."

But never a bit of dry bread did the cloth serve up.

"Well," said the *Lad*, "there's no help for it but to go to the *North Wind* again;" and away he went.

So he came to where the *North Wind* lived late in the afternoon.

"Good evening!" said the *Lad*.

"Good evening!" said the *North Wind*.

"I want my rights for that meal of ours which you took," said the *Lad*; "for, as for that cloth I got, it isn't worth a penny."

"I've got no meal," said the *North Wind*; "but yonder you have a ram which coins nothing but golden ducats as soon as you say to it: 'Ram, ram! make money!'"

So the *Lad* thought this a fine thing; but as it was too far to get home that day, he turned in for the night to the same inn where he had slept before.

Before he called for anything, he tried the truth of what the *North Wind* had said of the ram, and found it all right; but, when the landlord saw that, he thought it was a famous ram, and, when the *Lad* had fallen asleep, he took another which couldn't coin gold ducats, and changed the two.

Next morning off went the *Lad;* and when he got home to his mother, he said:

"After all, the *North Wind* is a jolly fellow; for now he has given me a ram which can coin golden ducats if I only say: 'Ram, ram! make money!'"

"All very true, I daresay," said his mother; "but I shan't believe any such stuff until I see the ducats made."

"Ram, ram! make money!" said the *Lad;* but if the ram made anything, it wasn't money.

So the *Lad* went back again to the *North Wind*, and blew him up, and said the ram was worth nothing, and he must have his rights for the meal.

"Well!" said the *North Wind;* "I've nothing else to give you but that old stick in the corner yonder; but its a stick of that kind that if you say: 'Stick, stick! lay on!' it lays on till you say: 'Stick, stick! now stop!'"

So, as the way was long, the *Lad* turned in this night too to the landlord; but as he could pretty well guess how things stood as to the cloth and the ram, he lay down at once on the bench and began to snore, as if he were asleep.

Now the landlord, who easily saw that the stick must be worth something, hunted up one which was like it, and when he heard the lad snore, was going to change the two; but, just as the landlord was about to take it, the *Lad* bawled out:

"Stick, stick! lay on!"

So the stick began to beat the landlord, till he jumped over chairs, and tables, and benches, and yelled and roared:

"Oh my! oh my! bid the stick be still, else it will beat me to death, and you shall have back both your cloth and your ram."

When the *Lad* thought the landlord had got enough, he said:

"Stick, stick! now stop!"

Then he took the cloth and put it into his pocket, and went home with his stick in his hand, leading the ram by a cord round its horns; and so he got his rights for the meal he had lost.

THE THREE PRINCESSES OF WHITELAND

ONCE on a time there was a fisherman who lived close by a palace, and fished for the *King's* table. One day when he was out fishing he just caught nothing. Do what he would—however he tried with bait and angle—there was never a sprat on his hook. But when the day was far spent a head bobbed up out of the water, and said:

"If I may have what your wife bears under her girdle, you shall catch fish enough."

So the man answered boldly, "Yes;" for he did not know that his wife was going to have a child. After that, as was like enough, he caught plenty of fish of all kinds. But when he got home at night and told his story, how he had got all that fish, his wife fell a-weeping and moaning, and was beside herself for the promise which her husband had made, for she said, "I bear a babe under my girdle."

Well, the story soon spread, and came up to the castle; and when the *King* heard the woman's grief and its cause, he sent down to say he would take care of the child, and see if he couldn't save it.

So the months went on and on, and when her time came the fisher's wife had a boy; so the king took it at once, and brought it up as his own son, until the lad grew up. Then he begged leave one day to go out fishing with his father; he had such a mind to go, he said. At first the *King* wouldn't hear of it, but at last the lad had his way, and went. So he and his father were out the whole day, and all went right and well till they landed at night. Then the lad remembered he had left his handkerchief, and went to look for it; but as soon as ever he got into the boat, it began to move off with him at such speed that the water roared under the bow, and all the lad could do in rowing against it with the oars was no use; so he went and went the whole night, and at last he came to a white strand, far far away.

There he went ashore, and when he had walked about a bit, an old, old man met him, with a long white beard.

"What's the name of this land?" asked the lad.

"Whiteland," said the man, who went on to ask the lad whence he came, and what he was going to do. So the lad told him all.

"Aye, aye!" said the man; "now when you have walked a little farther along the strand here, you'll come to three *Princesses*, whom you will see standing in the earth up to their necks, with only their heads out. Then the first—she is the eldest—will call out and beg you so prettily to come and help her; and the second will do the same; to neither of these shall you go; make haste past them, as if you neither saw nor heard anything. But the third you shall go to, and do what she asks. If you do this, you'll have good luck—that's all."

When the lad came to the first *Princess*, she called out to him, and begged him so prettily to come to her, but he passed on as though he saw her not. In the same way he passed by the second; but to the third he went straight up.

"If you'll do what I bid you," she said, "you may have which of us you please."

"Yes;" he was willing enough; so she told him how three *Trolls* had set them down in the earth there; but before they had lived in the castle up among the trees.

"Now," she said, "you must go into that castle, and let the *Trolls* whip you each one night for each of us. If you can bear that, you'll set us free."

Well, the lad said he was ready to try.

"When you go in," the *Princess* went on to say, "you'll see two lions standing at the gate; but if you'll only go right in the middle between them they'll do you no harm. Then go straight on into a little dark room, and make your bed. Then the *Troll* will come to whip you; but if you take the flask which hangs on the wall, and rub yourself with the ointment that's in it, wherever his lash falls, you'll be as sound as ever. Then grasp the sword that hangs by the side of the flask and strike the *Troll* dead."

Yes, he did as the *Princess* told him; he passed in the midst between the lions, as if he hadn't seen them, and went straight into the little room, and there he lay down to sleep. The first night there came a *Troll* with three

"You'll come to three Princesses, whom you will see standing in the earth up to their necks, with only their heads out." *Page 87*

heads and three rods, and whipped the lad soundly; but he stood it till the *Troll* was done; then he took the flask and rubbed himself, and grasped the sword and slew the *Troll*.

So, when he went out next morning, the *Princesses* stood out of the earth up to their waists.

The next night 'twas the same story over again, only this time the *Troll* had six heads and six rods, and he whipped him far worse than the first; but when he went out next morning, the *Princesses* stood out of the earth as far as the knee.

The third night there came a *Troll* that had nine heads and nine rods, and he whipped and flogged the lad so long that he fainted away; then the

Troll took him up and dashed him against the wall; but the shock brought down the flask, which fell on the lad, burst, and spilled the ointment all over him, and so he became as strong and sound as ever again. Then he wasn't slow; he grasped the sword and slew the *Troll*; and next morning when he went out of the castle the *Princesses* stood before him with all their bodies out of the earth. So he took the youngest for his *Queen*, and lived well and happily with her for some time.

At last he began to long to go home for a little to see his parents. His *Queen* did not like this; but at last his heart was so set on it, and he longed and longed so much, there was no holding him back, so she said:

"One thing you must promise me. This—only to do what your father begs you to do, and not what mother wishes;" and that he promised.

Then she gave him a ring, which was of that kind that any one who wore it might wish two wishes. So he wished himself home, and when he got home his parents could not wonder enough what a grand man their son had become.

Now, when he had been at home some days, his mother wished him to go up to the palace and show the

King what a fine fellow he had come to be. But his father said:

"No! don't let him do that; if he does, we shan't have any more joy of him this time."

But it was no good, the mother begged and prayed so long that at last he went. So when he got up to the palace he was far braver, both in clothes and array, than the other king, who didn't quite like this, and at last he said:

"All very fine; but here you can see my *Queen*, what like she is, but I can't see yours: that I can't. Do you know, I scarce think she's so good-looking as mine."

"Would to Heaven," said the young *King*, "she were standing here, then you'd see what she was like." And that instant there she stood before them.

But she was very woeful, and said to him:

"Why did you not mind what I told you; and why did you not listen to what your father said? Now, I must away home, and as for you, you have had both your wishes."

With that she knitted a ring among his hair with her name on it, and wished herself home, and was off.

Then the young *King* was cut to the heart, and went, day out day in, thinking and thinking how he should get back to his *Queen*. "I'll just try," he thought, "if I can't learn where Whiteland lies;" and so he went out into the world to ask. So when he had gone a good way, he came to a high hill, and there he met one who was lord over all the beasts of the wood, for they all came home to him when he blew his horn; so the *King* asked if he knew where Whiteland was.

"No, I don't," said he, "but I'll ask my beasts." Then he blew his horn and called them, and asked if any of them knew where Whiteland lay. But there was no beast that knew.

So the man gave him a pair of snow-shoes.

"When you get on these," he said, "you'll come to my brother, who lives hundreds of miles off; he is lord over all the birds of the air. Ask him. When you reach his house, just turn the shoes so that the toes point this way, and they'll come home of themselves." So when the *King* reached the house, he turned the shoes as the lord of the beasts had said, and away they went home of themselves.

So he asked again after Whiteland, and the man called all the birds with a blast of his horn, and asked if any of them knew where Whiteland lay; but none of the birds knew. Now, long, long after the rest of the birds came an old eagle, which had been away ten round years, but he couldn't tell any more than the rest.

"Well, well," said the man, "I'll lend you a pair of snow-shoes, and, when you get them on, they'll carry you to my brother, who lives hundreds of miles off; he's lord of all the fish in the sea; you'd better ask him. But don't forget to turn the toes of the shoes this way."

The *King* was full of thanks, got on the shoes, and when he came to the man who was lord over the fish of the sea, he turned the toes round, and so off they went home like the other pair. After that, he asked again after Whiteland.

So the man called the fish with a blast, but no fish could tell where it lay. At last came an old pike, which they had great work to call home, he was such a way off. So when they asked him he said:

"Know it? I should think I did! I've been cook there ten years, and to-morrow I'm going there again; for now the queen of Whiteland, whose king is away, is going to wed another husband."

"Well!" said the man, "as this is so, I'll give you a bit of advice. Hereabouts, on a moor, stand three brothers, and here they have stood these hundred years, fighting about a hat, a cloak, and a pair of boots. If any one has these three things he can make himself invisible, and wish himself anywhere he pleases. You can tell them you wish to try the things, and, after that, you'll pass judgment between them, whose they shall be."

Yes! the *King* thanked the man, and went and did as he told him.

"What's all this?" he said to the brothers. "Why do you stand here fighting for ever and a day? Just let me try these things, and I'll give judgment whose they shall be."

They were very willing to do this; but, as soon as he had got the hat, cloak, and boots, he said:

"When we meet next time, I'll tell you my judgment," and with these words he wished himself away.

So as he went along up in the air, he came up with the North wind.

"Whither away?" roared the North Wind.

"To Whiteland," said the *King*; "and then he told him all that had befallen him.

"Ah," said the North Wind, "you go faster than I—you do; for you can go straight, while I have to puff and blow round every turn and corner. But when you get there, just place yourself on the stairs by the side of the door, and then I'll come storming in, as though I were going to blow down the whole castle. And then when the prince, who is to have your *Queen*, comes out to see what's the matter, just you take him by the collar and pitch him out of doors; then I'll look after him, and see if I can't carry him off."

Well, the *King* did as the North Wind said. He took his stand on the stairs, and when the North Wind came, storming and roaring, and took hold of the castle wall, so that it shook again, the prince came out to see what was the matter. But as soon as ever he came, the *King* caught him by the collar and pitched him out of doors, and then the North Wind caught him up and carried him off. So when there was an end of him, the *King* went into the castle, and at first his *Queen* didn't know him, he was so wan and thin, through wandering so far and being so woeful; but when he shewed her the ring, she was as glad as glad could be; and so the rightful wedding was held, and the fame of it spread far and wide.

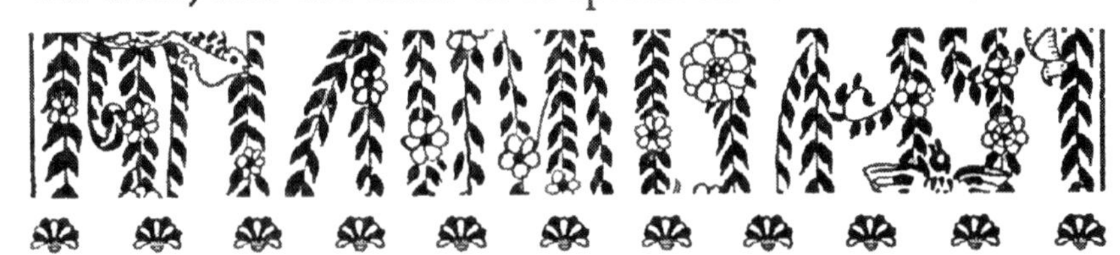

So the man gave him a pair of snow-shoes. *Page 92*

SORIA MORIA CASTLE

ONCE on a time there was a poor couple who had a son whose name was *Halvor*. Ever since he was a little boy he would turn his hand to nothing, but just sat there and groped about in the ashes. His father and mother often put him out to learn this trade or that, but *Halvor* could stay nowhere; for, when he had been there a day or two, he ran away from his master, and never stopped till he was sitting again in the ingle, poking about in the cinders.

Well, one day a skipper came, and asked *Halvor* if he hadn't a mind to be with him, and go to sea, and see strange lands. Yes, *Halvor* would like that very much; so he wasn't long in getting himself ready.

How long they sailed I'm sure I can't tell; but the end of it was, they fell into a great storm, and when it was blown over, and it got still again, they couldn't tell where they were; for they had been driven away to a strange coast, which none of them knew anything about.

Well, as there was just no wind at all, they stayed lying wind-bound there, and *Halvor* asked the skipper's leave to go on shore and look about him; he would sooner go, he said, than lie there and sleep.

"Do you think now you're fit to show yourself before folk," said the skipper, "why, you've no clothes but those rags you stand in?"

But *Halvor* stuck to his own, and so at last he got leave, but he was to be sure and come back as soon as ever it began to blow. So off he went and found a lovely land; wherever he came there were fine large flat cornfields and rich meads, but he couldn't catch a glimpse of a living soul. Well, it began to blow, but *Halvor* thought he hadn't seen enough yet, and he wanted to walk a little farther just to see if he couldn't meet any folk. So after a while he came to a broad high road, so smooth and even, you might easily roll an egg along it. *Halvor* followed this, and when evening drew on he saw a great castle ever so far off, from which the sunbeams shone. So as he had now walked the whole day and hadn't taken a bit to eat with him, he was as hungry as a hunter, but still the nearer he came to the castle, the more afraid he got.

In the castle kitchen a great fire was blazing, and *Halvor* went into it, but such a kitchen he had never seen in all his born days. It was so grand and fine; there were vessels of silver and vessels of gold, but still never a living soul. So when *Halvor* had stood there a while and no one came out, he went and opened a door, and there inside sat a *Princess* who span upon a spinning-wheel.

"Nay, nay, now!" she called out, "dare Christian folk come hither? But now you'd best be off about your business, if you don't want the *Troll* to gobble you up; for here lives a *Troll* with three heads."

"All one to me," said the lad, "I'd be just as glad to hear he had four heads beside; I'd like to see what kind of fellow he is. As for going, I won't go at all. I've done no harm; but meat you must get me, for I'm almost starved to death."

When *Halvor* had eaten his fill, the *Princess* told him to try if he could brandish the sword that hung against the wall; no, he couldn't brandish it, he couldn't even lift it up.

"Oh!" said the *Princess*, "now you must go and take a pull of that flask that hangs by its side; that's what the *Troll* does every time he goes out to use the sword."

So *Halvor* took a pull, and in the twinkling of an eye he could brandish the sword like nothing; and now he thought it high time the *Troll* came; and lo! just then up came the *Troll* puffing and blowing. *Halvor* jumped behind the door.

"HUTETU," said the *Troll*, as he put his head in at the door, "what a smell of Christian man's blood!"

"Aye," said *Halvor*, "you'll soon know that to your cost," and with that he hewed off all his heads.

Now the *Princess* was so glad that she was free, she both danced and sang, but then all at once she called her sisters to mind, and so she said:

"Would my sisters were free too!"

"Where are they?" asked *Halvor*.

Well, she told him all about it; one was taken away by a *Troll* to his Castle which lay fifty miles off, and the other by another *Troll* to his Castle which was fifty miles further still.

"But now," she said, "you must first help me to get this ugly carcass out of the house."

Yes, *Halvor* was so strong he swept everything away, and made it all clean and tidy in no time. So they had a good and happy time of it, and next morning he set off at peep of grey dawn; he could take no rest by the way, but ran and walked the whole day. When he first saw the Castle he got a little afraid; it was far grander than the first, but here too there wasn't a living soul to be seen. So *Halvor* went into the kitchen, and didn't stop there either, but went straight further on into the house.

"Nay, nay," called out the *Princess*, "dare Christian folk come hither? I don't know I'm sure how long it is since I came here, but in all that time I haven't seen a Christian man. 'Twere best you saw how to get away as fast as you came; for here lives a *Troll* who has six heads."

"I shan't go," said *Halvor*, "if he has six heads besides."

"He'll take you up and swallow you down alive," said the *Princess*.

But it was no good, *Halvor* wouldn't go; he wasn't at all afraid of the *Troll*, but meat and drink he must have, for he was half starved after his long journey. Well, he got as much of that as he wished, but then the *Princess* wanted him to be off again.

"No," said *Halvor*, "I won't go, I've done no harm, and I've nothing to be afraid about."

"He won't stay to ask that," said the *Princess*, "for he'll take you without law or leave; but as you won't go, just try if you can brandish that sword yonder, which the *Troll* wields in war."

He couldn't brandish it, and then the *Princess* said he must take a pull at the flask which hung by its side, and when he had done that he could brandish it.

Just then back came the *Troll*, and he was both stout and big, so that he had to go sideways to get through the door. When the *Troll* got his first head in he called out:

"HUTETU, what a smell of Christian man's blood!"

But that very moment *Halvor* hewed off his first head, and so on all the rest as they popped in. The *Princess* was overjoyed, but just then she came to think of her sisters, and wished out loud they were free. *Halvor* thought that might easily be done, and wanted to be off at once; but first he had to help the *Princess* to get the *Troll's* carcass out of the way, and so he could only set out next morning.

It was a long way to the Castle, and he had to walk fast and run hard to reach it in time; but about nightfall he saw the Castle, which was far finer and grander than either of the others. This time he wasn't the least afraid, but walked straight through the kitchen, and into the Castle. There sat a *Princess* who was so pretty, there was no end to her loveliness. She too like the others told him there hadn't been Christian folk there ever since she came thither, and bade him go away again, else the *Troll* would swallow him alive, and do you know, she said, he has nine heads.

"Aye, aye," said *Halvor*, "if he had nine other heads, and nine other heads still, I won't go away," and so he stood fast before the stove. The *Princess* kept on begging him so prettily to go away, lest the *Troll* should gobble him up, but *Halvor* said:

"Let him come as soon as he likes."

So she gave him the *Troll's* sword, and bade him take a pull at the flask, that he might be able to brandish and wield it.

Just then back came the *Troll* puffing and blowing and tearing along. He was far bigger and stouter than the other two, and he too had to go on one side to get through the door. So when he got his first head in, he said as the others had said:

"HUTETU, what a smell of Christian man's blood!"

That very moment *Halvor* hewed off the first head and then all the rest; but the last was the toughest of them all, and it was the hardest bit of work *Halvor* had to do, to get it hewn off, although he knew very well he had strength enough to do it.

So all the *Princesses* came together to that Castle, which was called *Soria Moria Castle*, and they were glad and happy as they had never been in all their lives before,

and they all were fond of *Halvor* and *Halvor* of them, and he might choose the one he liked best for his bride; but the youngest was fondest of him of all the three.

But there after a while, *Halvor* went about, and was so strange and dull and silent. Then the Princesses asked him what he lacked, and if he didn't like to live with them any longer? Yes, he did, for they had enough and to spare, and he was well off in every way, but still somehow or other he did so long to go home, for his father and mother were alive, and them he had such a great wish to see.

Well, they thought that might be done easily enough.

The King went into the Castle, and at first his Queen didn't know him, he was so wan and thin, through wandering so far and being so woeful. *Page* 95

"You shall go thither and come back hither, safe and unscathed, if you will only follow our advice," said the *Princesses.*

Yes, he'd be sure to mind all they said. So they dressed him up till he was as grand as a king's son, and then they set a ring on his finger, and that was such a ring, he could wish himself thither and hither with it; but they told him to be sure and not take it off, and not to name their names, for there would be an end of all his bravery, and then he'd never see them more.

"If I only stood at home I'd be glad," said *Halvor;* and it was done as he had wished. Then stood *Halvor* at his father's cottage door before he knew a word about it. Now it was about dusk at even, and so, when they saw such a grand stately lord walk in, the old couple got so afraid they began to bow and scrape. Then *Halvor* asked if he couldn't stay there, and have a lodging there that night. No; that he couldn't.

"We can't do it at all," they said, "for we haven't this thing or that thing which such a lord is used to have; 'twere best your lordship went up to the farm, no long way off, for you can see the chimneys, and there they have lots of everything."

Halvor wouldn't hear of it—he wanted to stop; but the old couple stuck to their own, that he had better go to the farmer's; there he would get both meat and drink; as for them, they hadn't even a chair to offer him to sit down on.

"No," said *Halvor*, "I won't go up there till to-morrow early, but let me just stay here to-night; worst come to the worst, I can sit in the chimney corner."

Well, they couldn't say anything against that; so *Halvor* sat down by the ingle, and began to poke about in the ashes, just as he used to do when he lay at home in old days, and stretched his lazy bones.

Well, they chattered and talked about many things; and they told *Halvor* about this thing and that; and so he asked them if they had never had any children.

Yes, yes, they had once a lad whose name was *Halvor*, but they didn't know whither he had wandered; they couldn't even tell whether he were dead or alive.

"Couldn't it be me, now?" said *Halvor*.

"Let me see; I could tell him well enough," said the old wife, and rose up. "Our *Halvor* was so lazy and dull, he never did a thing; and besides, he was so ragged, that one tatter took hold of the next tatter on him. No;

there never was the making of such a fine fellow in him as you are, master."

A little while after the old wife went to the hearth to poke up the fire, and when the blaze fell on *Halvor's* face, just as when he was at home of old poking about in the ashes, she knew him at once.

"Ah! but it is you after all, *Halvor?*" she cried; and then there was such joy for the old couple, there was no end to it; and he was forced to tell how he had fared, and the old dame was so fond and proud of him, nothing would do but he must go up at once to the farmer's, and show himself to the lassies, who had always looked down on him. And off she went first, and *Halvor* followed after. So, when she got up there, she told them all how *Halvor* had come home again, and now they should only just see how grand he was, for, said she, "he looks like nothing but a King's son."

"All very fine," said the lassies, and tossed up their heads. "We'll be bound he's just the same beggarly ragged boy he always was."

Just then in walked *Halvor*, and then the lassies were all so taken aback, they forgot their sarks in the ingle, where they were sitting darning their clothes, and ran out in their smocks. Well, when they were got back again, they were so shamefaced they scarce dared look at *Halvor*, towards whom they had always been proud and haughty.

"Aye, aye," said *Halvor*, "you always thought yourselves so pretty and neat, no one could come near you; but now you should just see the eldest *Princess* I have set free; against her you look just like milkmaids, and the midmost is prettier still; but the youngest, who is my sweetheart, she's fairer than both sun and moon. Would to Heaven they were only here," said *Halvor*, "then you'd see what you would see."

He had scarce uttered these words before there they stood, but then he felt so sorry, for now what they had said came into his mind. Up at the farm there was a great feast got ready for the *Princesses*, and much was made of them, but they wouldn't stop there.

"No, we want to go down to your father and mother," they said to *Halvor*; "and so we'll go out now and look about us."

So he went down with them, and they came to a great lake just outside the farm. Close by the water was such a lovely green bank; here the *Princesses* said they would sit and rest a while; they thought it so sweet to sit down and look over the water.

So they sat down there, and when they had sat a while the youngest *Princess* said:

"I may as well comb your hair a little, *Halvor*."

Well, *Halvor* laid his head on her lap, and she combed his bonny locks, and it wasn't long before *Halvor* fell fast asleep. Then she took the ring from his finger, and put another in its stead; and she said:

"Now hold me all together! and now would we were all in *Soria Moria Castle*."

So when *Halvor* woke up, he could very well tell that he had lost the *Princesses*, and began to weep and wail; and he was so downcast, they couldn't comfort him at all. In spite of all his father and mother said, he wouldn't stop there, but took farewell of them, and said he was safe not to see them again; for if he couldn't find the *Princesses* again, he thought it not worth while to live.

Well, he had still about sixty pounds left, so he put them into his pocket, and set out on his way. So, when he had walked a while, he met a man with a tidy horse, and he wanted to buy it, and began to chaffer with the man.

"Aye," said the man, "to tell the truth, I never thought of selling him; but if we could strike a bargain perhaps—"

"What do you want for him?" asked *Halvor*.

"I didn't give much for him, nor is he worth much; he 's a brave horse to ride, but he can't draw at all; still he 's strong enough to carry your knapsack and you too, turn and turn about," said the man.

At last they agreed on the price, and *Halvor* laid the knapsack on him, and so he walked a bit, and rode a bit, turn and turn about. At night he came to a green plain where stood a great tree, at the roots of which he sat down. There he let the horse loose, but he didn't lie down to sleep, but opened his knapsack and took a meal. At peep of day off he set again, for he could take no rest. So he rode and walked and walked and rode the whole day through the wide wood, where there were so many green spots and glades that shone so bright and lovely between the trees. He didn't know at all where he was or whither he was going, but he gave himself no more time to rest than when his horse cropped a bit of grass, and he took a snack out of his knapsack when they came to one of those green glades. So he went on walking and riding by turns, and as for the wood there seemed to be no end to it.

But at dusk the next day he saw a light gleaming away through the trees.

"Would there were folk hereaway," thought *Halvor*, "that I might warm myself a bit and get a morsel to keep body and soul together."

When he got up to it he saw the light came from a wretched little hut, and through the window he saw an old old, couple inside. They were as grey-headed as a pair of doves, and the old wife had such a nose! why, it was so long she used it for a poker to stir the fire as she sat in the ingle.

"Good evening," said *Halvor*.

"Good evening," said the old wife.

"But what errand can you have in coming hither?" she went on, "for no Christian folk have been here these hundred years and more."

Well, *Halvor* told her all about himself, and how he wanted to get to *Soria Moria Castle*, and asked if she knew the way thither.

"No," said the old wife, "that I don't, but see now, here comes the Moon, I'll ask her, she'll know all about it, for doesn't she shine on everything?"

So when the Moon stood clear and bright over the tree-tops, the old wife went out.

"THOU MOON, THOU MOON," she screamed, "canst thou tell me the way to *Soria Moria Castle?*"

"No," said the Moon, "that I can't, for the last time I shone there a cloud stood before me."

"Wait a bit still," said the old wife to *Halvor*, "bye and bye comes the West Wind; he's sure to know it, for he puffs and blows round every corner."

"Nay, nay," said the old wife when she went out again, "you don't mean to say you've got a horse too; just turn the poor beastie loose in our 'toun,' and don't let him stand there and starve to death at the door."

Then she ran on:

The six brothers riding out to woo. Page 117

"But won't you swop him away to me?—we've got an old pair of boots here, with which you can take twenty miles at each stride; those you shall have for your horse, and so you'll get all the sooner to *Soria Moria Castle*."

That *Halvor* was willing to do at once; and the old wife was so glad at having the horse, she was ready to dance and skip for joy.

"For now," she said, "I shall be able to ride to church. I, too, think of that."

As for *Halvor*, he had no rest, and wanted to be off at once, but the old wife said there was no hurry.

"Lie down on the bench with you and sleep a bit, for we've no bed to offer you, and I'll watch and wake you when the West Wind comes."

So after a while up came the West Wind, roaring and howling along till the walls creaked and groaned again.

Out ran the old wife.

"THOU WEST WIND, THOU WEST WIND! Canst thou tell me the way to *Soria Moria Castle?* Here's one who wants to get thither."

"Yes, I know it very well," said the West Wind, "and now I'm just off thither to dry clothes for the wedding that's to be; if he's swift of foot he can go along with me."

Out ran *Halvor.*

"You'll have to stretch your legs if you mean to keep up," said the West Wind.

So off he set over field and hedge, and hill and fell, and *Halvor* had hard work to keep up.

"Well," said the West Wind, "now I've no time to stay with you any longer, for I've got to go away yonder and tear down a strip of spruce wood first before I go to the bleaching-ground to dry the clothes; but if you go alongside the hill you'll come to a lot of lassies standing washing clothes, and then you've not far to go to *Soria Moria Castle.*"

In a little while *Halvor* came upon the lassies who stood washing, and they asked if he had seen anything of the West Wind who was to come and dry the clothes for the wedding.

"Aye, aye, that I have," said *Halvor*, "he's only gone to tear down a strip of spruce wood. It'll not be long before he's here," and then he asked them the way to *Soria Moria Castle.*

So they put him into the right way, and when he got to the Castle it was full of folk and horses; so full it made one giddy to look at them. But *Halvor* was so ragged and torn from having followed the West Wind through bush and brier and bog, that he kept on one side, and wouldn't show himself till the last day when the bridal feast was to be.

So when all, as was then right and fitting, were to drink the bride and bridegroom's health and wish them luck, and when the cupbearer was to drink to them all again, both knights and squires, last of all he came in turn to *Halvor*. He drank their health, but let the ring which the *Princess* had put upon his finger as he lay by the lake fall into the glass, and bade the cupbearer go and greet the bride and hand her the glass.

Then up rose the *Princess* from the board at once.

"Who is most worthy to have one of us," she said, "he that has set us free, or he that here sits by me as bridegroom?"

Well they all said there could be but one voice and will as to that, and when *Halvor* heard that he wasn't long in throwing off his beggar's rags, and arraying himself as bridegroom.

"Aye, aye, here is the right one after all," said the youngest *Princess* as soon as she saw him, and so she tossed the other one out of the window, and held her wedding with *Halvor*.

THE GIANT WHO HAD NO HEART IN HIS BODY

ONCE on a time there was a *King* who had *seven sons*, and he loved them so much that he could never bear to be without them all at once, but one must always be with him. Now, when they were grown up, six were to set off to woo, but as for the youngest, his father kept him at home, and the others were to bring back a princess for him to the palace. So the *King* gave the six the finest clothes you ever set eyes on, so fine that the light gleamed from them a long way off, and each had his horse, which cost many, many hundred pounds, and so they set off. Now, when they had been to many palaces, and seen many princesses, at last they came to a *King* who had *six daughters;* such lovely king's daughters they had never seen, and so they fell to wooing them, each one, and when they had got them for sweethearts, they set off home again, but they quite forgot that they were to bring back with them a sweetheart for *Boots*, their brother, who stayed at home, for they were over head and ears in love with their own sweethearts.

But when they had gone a good bit on their way, they passed close by a steep hill-side, like a wall, where the *Giant's* house was, and there the *Giant* came out, and set his eyes upon them, and turned them all into stone, princes and princesses and all. Now the *King* waited and waited for his *six sons*, but the more he waited, the longer they stayed away; so he fell into great trouble, and said he should never know what it was to be glad again.

"And if I had not you left," he said to *Boots*, "I would live no longer, so full of sorrow am I for the loss of your brothers."

"Well, but now I've been thinking to ask your leave to set out and find them again; that's what I'm thinking of," said *Boots.*

"Nay, nay!" said his father; "that leave you shall never get, for then you would stay away too."

But *Boots* had set his heart upon it; go he would; and he begged and prayed so long that the *King* was forced to let him go. Now, you must know the *King* had no other horse to give *Boots* but an old broken-down jade, for his six other sons and their train had carried off all his horses; but *Boots* did not care a pin for that, he sprang up on his sorry old steed.

"Farewell, father," said he; "I'll come back, never fear, and like enough I shall bring my six brothers back with me;" and with that he rode off.

So, when he had ridden a while, he came to a *Raven*, which lay in the road and flapped its wings, and was not able to get out of the way, it was so starved.

"Oh, dear friend," said the *Raven*, "give me a little food, and I'll help you again at your utmost need."

"I haven't much food," said the *Prince*, "and I don't see how you'll ever be able to help me much; but still I can spare you a little. I see you want it."

So he gave the raven some of the food he had brought with him.

Now, when he had gone a bit further, he came to a brook, and in the brook lay a great *Salmon*, which had got upon a dry place and dashed itself about, and could not get into the water again.

"Oh, dear friend," said the *Salmon* to the *Prince*; "shove me out into the water again, and I'll help you again at your utmost need."

"Well!" said the *Prince*, "the help you'll give me will not be great, I daresay, but it's a pity you should lie there and choke;" and with that he shot the fish out into the stream again.

After that he went a long, long way, and there met him a *Wolf*, which was so famished that it lay and crawled along the road on its belly.

"Dear friend, do let me have your horse," said the *Wolf*; "I'm so hungry the wind whistles through my ribs; I've had nothing to eat these two years."

"No," said *Boots*, "this will never do; first I came to a raven, and I was forced to give him my food; next I came to a salmon, and him I had to help into the water again; and now you will have my horse. It can't be done, that it can't, for then I should have nothing to ride on."

"On that island stands a church; in that church is a well; in that well swims a duck." *Page 126*

"Nay, dear friend, but you can help me," said *Graylegs* the wolf; "you can ride upon my back, and I'll help you again in your utmost need."

"Well! the help I shall get from you will not be great, I'll be bound," said the *Prince*; "but you may take my horse, since you are in such need."

So when the *Wolf* had eaten the horse, *Boots* took the bit and put it into the *Wolf's* jaw, and laid the saddle on his back; and now the *Wolf* was so strong, after what he had got inside, that he set off with the *Prince* like nothing. So fast he had never ridden before.

"When we have gone a bit farther," said *Graylegs*, "I'll show you the *Giant's* house."

So after a while they came to it.

"See, here is the *Giant's* house," said the *Wolf*; "and see, here are your six brothers, whom the *Giant* has turned into stone; and see, here are their six brides, and away yonder is the door, and in that door you must go."

"Nay, but I daren't go in," said the *Prince*; "he'll take my life."

"No! no!" said the *Wolf*; "when you get in you'll find a *Princess*, and she'll tell you what to do to make an end of the *Giant*. Only mind and do as she bids you."

Well! *Boots* went in, but, truth to say, he was very much afraid. When he came in the *Giant* was away, but in one of the rooms sat the *Princess*, just as the *Wolf* had said, and so lovely a princess *Boots* had never yet set eyes on.

"Oh! heaven help you! whence have you come?" said the *Princess*, as she saw him; "it will surely be your death. No one can make an end of the *Giant* who lives here, for he has no heart in his body."

"Well! well!" said *Boots*; "but now that I am here, I may as well try what I can do with him; and I will see if I can't free my brothers, who are standing turned to stone out of doors; and you, too, I will try to save, that I will."

"Well, if you must, you must," said the *Princess*; "and so let us see if we can't hit on a plan. Just creep under the bed yonder, and mind and listen to what he and I talk about. But, pray, do lie as still as a mouse."

So he crept under the bed, and he had scarce got well underneath it, before the *Giant* came.

"Ha!" roared the *Giant*, "what a smell of Christian blood there is in the house!"

"Yes, I know there is," said the *Princess*, "for there came a magpie flying with a man's bone, and let it fall down the chimney. I made all the haste I could to get it out, but all one can do, the smell doesn't go off so soon."

So the *Giant* said no more about it, and when night came, they went to bed. After they had lain a while, the *Princess* said:

"There is one thing I'd be so glad to ask you about, if I only dared."

"What thing is that?" asked the *Giant*.

"Only where it is you keep your heart, since you don't carry it about you," said the *Princess*.

"Ah! that's a thing you've no business to ask about; but if you must know, it lies under the door-sill," said the *Giant*.

"Ho! ho!" said *Boots* to himself under the bed, "then we'll soon see if we can't find it."

Next morning the *Giant* got up cruelly early, and strode off to the wood; but he was hardly out of the house before *Boots* and the *Princess* set to work to look under the door-sill for his heart; but the more they dug, and the more they hunted, the more they couldn't find it.

"He has baulked us this time," said the *Princess*, "but we'll try him once more."

So she picked all the prettiest flowers she could find, and strewed them over the door-sill, which they had laid in its right place again; and when the time came for the *Giant* to come home again, *Boots* crept under the bed. Just as he was well under, back came the *Giant*.

Snuff—snuff, went the *Giant's* nose. "My eyes and limbs, what a smell of Christian blood there is in here," said he.

"I know there is," said the *Princess*, "for there came a magpie flying with a man's bone in his bill, and let it fall down the chimney. I made as much haste as I could to get it out, but I daresay it's that you smell."

So the *Giant* held his peace, and said no more about it. A little while after, he asked who it was that had strewed flowers about the door-sill.

"Oh, I, of course," said the *Princess*.

"And, pray, what's the meaning of all this?" said the *Giant*.

"Ah!" said the *Princess*, "I'm so fond of you that I couldn't help strewing them, when I knew that your heart lay under there."

"You don't say so," said the *Giant;* "but after all it doesn't lie there at all."

So when they went to bed again in the evening, the *Princess* asked the *Giant* again where his heart was, for she said she would so like to know.

"Well," said the *Giant*, "if you must know, it lies away yonder in the cupboard against the wall."

"So, so!" thought *Boots* and the *Princess;* "then we'll soon try to find it."

Next morning the *Giant* was away early, and strode off to the wood, and so soon as he was gone *Boots* and the *Princess* were in the cupboard hunting for his heart, but the more they sought for it, the less they found it.

"Well," said the *Princess*, "we'll just try him once more."

So she decked out the cupboard with flowers and garlands, and when the time came for the *Giant* to come home, *Boots* crept under the bed again.

Then back came the Giant.

Snuff—snuff! "My eyes and limbs, what a smell of Christian blood there is in here!"

"I know there is," said the *Princess;* "for a little while since there came a magpie flying with a man's bone in his bill, and let it fall down the chimney. I made all the haste I could to get it out of the house again; but after all my pains, I daresay it's that you smell."

When the *Giant* heard that, he said no more about it; but a little while after, he saw how the cupboard was all decked about with flowers and garlands; so he asked who it was that had done that? Who could it be but the *Princess?*

"And, pray, what's the meaning of all this tom-foolery?" asked the *Giant.*

"Oh, I'm so fond of you, I couldn't help doing it when I knew that your heart lay there," said the *Princess.*

"How can you be so silly as to believe any such thing?" said the *Giant.*

"Oh yes; how can I help believing it, when you say it?" said the *Princess.*

"You're a goose," said the *Giant;* "where my heart is, you will never come."

"Well," said the *Princess;* "but for all that, 'twould be such a pleasure to know where it really lies."

Then the poor *Giant* could hold out no longer, but was forced to say:

"Far, far away in a lake lies an island; on that island stands a church; in that church is a well; in that well swims a duck; in that duck there is an egg, and in that egg there lies my heart,—you darling!"

In the morning early, while it was still grey dawn, the *Giant* strode off to the wood.

"Yes! now I must set off too," said *Boots*; "if I only knew how to find the way." He took a long, long farewell of the *Princess*, and when he got out of the *Giant's* door, there stood the *Wolf* waiting for him. So *Boots* told him all that had happened inside the house, and said now he wished to ride to the well in the church, if he only knew the way. So the *Wolf* bade him jump on his back, he'd soon find the way; and away they went, till the wind whistled after them, over hedge and field, over hill and dale. After they had travelled many, many days, they came at last to the lake. Then the *Prince* did not know how to get over it, but the *Wolf* bade him only not be afraid, but stick on, and so he jumped into the lake with the *Prince* on his back, and swam over to the island. So they came to the church; but the church keys hung high, high up on the top of the tower, and at first the *Prince* did not know how to get them down.

"You must call on the raven," said the *Wolf*.

So the *Prince* called on the raven, and in a trice the raven came, and flew up and fetched the keys, and so the *Prince* got into the church. But when he came to the well, there lay the duck, and swam about backwards and forwards, just as the *Giant* had said. So the *Prince* stood and coaxed it, till it came to him, and he grasped it in his hand; but just as he lifted it up from the water the duck dropped the egg into the well, and then *Boots* was beside himself to know how to get it out again.

"Well, now you must call on the salmon to be sure," said the *Wolf*; and the king's son called on the salmon, and the salmon came and fetched up the egg from the bottom of the well.

Then the *Wolf* told him to squeeze the egg, and as soon as ever he squeezed it the *Giant* screamed out.

"Squeeze it again," said the *Wolf*; and when the *Prince* did so, the *Giant* screamed still more piteously, and begged and prayed so prettily to be spared, saying he would do all that the *Prince* wished if he would only not squeeze his heart in two.

"Tell him, if he will restore to life again your six brothers and their brides, whom he has turned to stone, you will spare his life," said the *Wolf*. Yes, the *Giant*

He took a long, long farewell of the Princess, and when he got out of the Giant's door, there stood the Wolf waiting for him. Page 127

was ready to do that, and he turned the six brothers into king's sons again, and their brides into king's daughters.

"Now, squeeze the egg in two," said the *Wolf*. So *Boots* squeezed the egg to pieces, and the *Giant* burst at once.

Now, when he had made an end of the *Giant*, *Boots* rode back again on the *Wolf* to the *Giant's* house, and there stood all his six brothers alive and merry, with their brides. Then *Boots* went into the hill-side after his bride, and so they all set off home again to their father's house. And you may fancy how glad the old king was when he saw all his seven sons come back, each with his bride—"But the loveliest bride of all is the bride of *Boots*, after all," said the king, "and he shall sit uppermost at the table, with her by his side."

So he sent out, and called a great wedding-feast, and the mirth was both loud and long, and if they have not done feasting, why, they are still at it.

THE PRINCESS ON THE GLASS HILL

ONCE on a time there was a man who had a meadow, which lay high up on the hill-side, and in the meadow was a barn, which he had built to keep his hay in. Now, I must tell you, there hadn't been much in the barn for the last year or two, for every St. John's night, when the grass stood greenest and deepest, the meadow was eaten down to the very ground the next morning, just as if a whole drove of sheep had been there feeding on it over night. This happened once, and it happened twice; so at last the man grew weary of losing his crop of hay, and said to his sons—for he had three of them, and the youngest was nicknamed *Boots*, of course—that now one of them must go and sleep in the barn in the outlying field when St. John's night came, for it was too good a joke that his grass should be eaten, root and blade, this year, as it had been the last two years. So whichever of them went must keep a sharp look-out; that was what their father said.

Well, the eldest son was ready to go and watch the meadow; trust him for looking after the grass! It shouldn't be his fault if man or beast, or the fiend himself, got a blade of grass. So, when evening came, he set off to the barn, and lay down to sleep; but a little on in the night came such a clatter, and such an earthquake, that walls and roof shook, and groaned, and creaked; then up jumped the lad, and took to his heels as fast as ever he could; nor dared he once look round till he reached home; and as for the hay, why it was eaten up this year just as it had been twice before.

The next St. John's night, the man said again, it would never do to lose all the grass in the outlying field year after year in this way, so one of his sons must just trudge off to watch it, and watch it well too. Well, the next oldest son was ready to try his luck, so he set off, and lay down to sleep in the barn as his brother had done before him; but as the night wore on, there came on a rumbling and quaking of the earth, worse even than on the last St. John's night, and when the lad heard it, he got frightened, and took to his heels as though he were running a race.

Next year the turn came to *Boots*; but when he made ready to go, the other two began to laugh and to make game of him, saying:

"You're just the man to watch the hay, that you are; you, who have done nothing all your life but sit in the ashes and toast yourself by the fire."

But *Boots* did not care a pin for their chattering, and stumped away as evening grew on, up the hill-side to the outlying field. There he went inside the barn and lay down; but in about an hour's time the barn began to groan and creak, so that it was dreadful to hear.

"Well," said *Boots* to himself, "if it isn't worse than this, I can stand it well enough."

A little while after came another creak and an earthquake, so that the litter in the barn flew about the lad's ears. "Oh!" said *Boots* to himself, "if it isn't worse than this, I daresay I can stand it out."

But just then came a third rumbling, and a third earthquake, so that the lad thought walls and roof were coming down on his head; but it passed off, and all was still as death about him.

"It'll come again, I'll be bound," thought *Boots*; but no, it didn't come again; still it was, and still it stayed; but after he had lain a little while, he heard a noise as if a horse were standing just outside the barn-door, and cropping the grass. He stole to the door, and peeped through a chink, and there stood a horse feeding away. So big, and fat, and grand a horse, *Boots* had never set eyes on; by his side on the grass lay a saddle and bridle, and a full set of armour for a knight, all of brass, so bright that the light gleamed from it.

"Ho, ho!" thought the lad; "it's you, is it, that eats up our hay? I'll soon put a spoke in your wheel, just see if I don't."

So he lost no time, but took the steel out of his tinder-box, and threw it over the horse; then it had no power to stir from the spot, and became so tame that the lad could do what he liked with it. So he got on its back, and rode off with it to a place which no one knew of, and there he put up the horse. When he got home, his brothers laughed and asked how he had fared?

"You didn't lie long in the barn, even if you had the heart to go so far as the field."

"Well," said *Boots*, "all I can say is, I lay in the barn till the sun rose, and neither saw nor heard anything; I can't think what there was in the barn to make you both so afraid."

"A pretty story," said his brothers; "but we'll soon see how you have watched the meadow;" so they set off; but when they reached it, there stood the grass as deep and thick as it had been over night.

Well, the next St. John's eve it was the same story over

again ; neither of the elder brothers dared to go out to the outlying field to watch the crop ; but *Boots*, he had the heart to go, and everything happened just as it had happened the year before. First a clatter and an earthquake, then a greater clatter and another earthquake, and so on a third time ; only this year the earthquakes were far worse than the year before. Then all at once everything was as still as death, and the lad heard how something was cropping the grass outside the barn-door, so he stole to the door, and peeped through a chink ; and what do you think he saw ? Why, another horse standing right up against the wall, and chewing and champing with might and main. It was far finer and fatter than that which came the year before, and it had a saddle on its back, and a bridle on its neck, and a full suit of mail for a knight lay by its side, all of silver, and as grand as you would wish to see.

"Ho, ho !" said *Boots* to himself ; "it's you that gobbles up our hay, is it ? I'll soon put a spoke in your wheel ;" and with that he took the steel out of his tinder-box, and threw it over the horse's crest, which stood as still as a lamb. Well, the lad rode this horse, too, to the hiding-place where he kept the other one, and after that he went home.

"I suppose you'll tell us," said one of his brothers, "there's a fine crop this year too, up in the hayfield."

"Well, so there is," said *Boots*; and off ran the others to see, and there stood the grass thick and deep, as it was the year before; but they didn't give *Boots* softer words for all that.

Now, when the third St. John's eve came, the two elder brothers still hadn't the heart to lie out in the barn and watch the grass, for they had got so scared at heart the nights they lay there before, that they couldn't get over the fright; but *Boots*, he dared to go; and, to make a very long story short, the very same thing happened this time as had happened twice before. Three earthquakes came, one after the other, each worse than the one which went before, and when the last came, the lad danced about with the shock from one barn wall to the other; and after that, all at once, it was still as death. Now when he had laid a little while, he heard something tugging away at the grass outside the barn, so he stole again to the door-chink, and peeped out, and there stood a horse close outside—far, far bigger and fatter than the two he had taken before.

"Ho, ho!" said the lad to himself, "it's you, is it, that comes here eating up our hay? I'll soon stop that—

When he had walked a day or so, a strange man met him. "Whither away?" asked the man. Page 149

"I'll soon put a spoke in your wheel." So he caught up his steel and threw it over his horse's neck, and in a trice it stood as if it were nailed to the ground, and *Boots* could do as he pleased with it. Then he rode off with it to the hiding-place where he kept the other two, and then went home. When he got home, his two brothers made game of him as they had done before, saying, they could see he had watched the grass well, for he looked for all the world as if he were walking in his sleep, and many other spiteful things they said, but *Boots* gave no heed to them, only asking them to go and see for themselves; and when they went, there stood the grass as fine and deep this time as it had been twice before.

Now, you must know that the king of the country where *Boots* lived had a daughter, whom he would only give to the man who could ride up over the hill of glass, for there was a high, high hill, all of glass, as smooth and slippery as ice, close by the *King's* palace. Upon the tip top of the hill the *King's* daughter was to sit, with three golden apples in her lap, and the man who could ride up and carry off the three golden apples, was to have half the kingdom, and the *Princess* to wife. This the *King* had stuck up on all the church-doors in his

realm, and had given it out in many other kingdoms besides. Now, this *Princess* was so lovely that all who set eyes on her fell over head and ears in love with her whether they would or no. So I needn't tell you how all the princes and knights who heard of her were eager to win her to wife, and half the kingdom beside; and how they came riding from all parts of the world on high prancing horses, and clad in the grandest clothes, for there wasn't one of them who hadn't made up his mind that he, and he alone, was to win the *Princess*.

So when the day of trial came, which the king had fixed, there was such a crowd of princes and knights under the *Glass Hill*, that it made one's head whirl to look at them, and everyone in the country who could even crawl along was off to the hill, for they were all eager to see the man who was to win the *Princess*. So the two elder brothers set off with the rest; but as for *Boots*, they said outright he shouldn't go with them, for if they were seen with such a dirty changeling, all begrimed with smut from cleaning their shoes and sifting cinders in the dust-hole, they said folk would make game of them.

"Very well," said *Boots*, "it's all one to me. I can go alone, and stand or fall by myself."

Now when the two brothers came to the *Hill of Glass*, the knights and princes were all hard at it, riding their horses till they were all in a foam; but it was no good, by my troth; for as soon as ever the horses set foot on the hill, down they slipped, and there wasn't one who could get a yard or two up; and no wonder, for the hill was as smooth as a sheet of glass, and as steep as a house-wall. But all were eager to have the *Princess* and half the kingdom. So they rode and slipped, and slipped and rode, and still it was the same story over again. At last all their horses were so weary that they could scarce lift a leg, and in such a sweat that the lather dripped from them, and so the knights had to give up trying any more. So the king was just thinking that he would proclaim a new trial for the next day, to see if they would have better luck, when all at once a knight came riding up on so brave a steed, that no one had ever seen the like of it in his born days, and the knight had mail of brass, and the horse a brass bit in his mouth, so bright that the sunbeams shone from it. Then all the others called out to him he might just as well spare himself the trouble of riding at the Hill, for it would lead to no good; but he gave no heed to them, and put his horse at the hill, and went up it like nothing for a good way, about a third of the height; and when he had got so far, he turned his horse round and rode down again. So lovely a knight the *Princess* thought she had never yet seen; and while he was riding, she sat and thought to herself:

"Would to heaven he might only come up and down the other side."

And when she saw him turning back, she threw down one of the golden apples after him, and it rolled down into his shoe. But when he got to the bottom of the hill, he rode off so fast that no one could tell what had become of him. That evening all the knights and princes were to go before the king, that he who had ridden so far up the hill might show the apple which the *Princess* had thrown, but there was no one who had anything to show. One after the other they all came, but not a man of them could show the apple.

At even the brothers of *Boots* came home too, and had such a long story to tell about the riding up the hill.

"First of all," they said, "there was not one of the whole lot who could get so much as a stride up; but at last came one who had a suit of brass mail, and a brass bridle and saddle, all so bright that the sun shone from them a mile off. He was a chap to ride, just! He rode a third of the way up the *Hill of Glass*, and he could easily have ridden the whole way up, if he chose; but he turned round and rode down, thinking, maybe, that was enough for once."

"Oh! I should so like to have seen him, that I should," said *Boots*, who sat by the fireside, and stuck his feet into the cinders, as was his wont.

"Oh!" said his brothers, "you would, would you? You look fit to keep company with such high lords, nasty beast that you are, sitting there amongst the ashes."

Next day the brothers were all for setting off again, and *Boots* begged them this time, too, to let him go with them and see the riding; but no, they wouldn't have him at any price, he was too ugly and nasty, they said.

"Well, well!" said *Boots;* "if I go at all, I must go by myself. I'm not afraid."

So when the brothers got to the *Hill of Glass*, all the princes and knights began to ride again, and you may fancy they had taken care to shoe their horses sharp; but it was no good—they rode and slipped, and slipped and rode, just as they had done the day before, and there was not one who could get so far as a yard up the hill. And when they had worn out their horses, so that they could not stir a leg, they were all forced to give it up as a bad job. So the king thought he might as well proclaim that the riding should take place the day after for the last time, just to give them one chance more; but all at once it came across his mind that he might as well wait a little longer, to see if the knight in brass mail would come this day too. Well, they saw nothing of him; but all at once came one riding on a steed, far, far braver and finer than that on which the knight in brass had ridden, and he had silver mail, and a silver saddle and bridle, all so bright that the sunbeams gleamed and glanced from them far away. Then the others shouted out to him again, saying, he might as well hold hard, and not try to ride up the hill, for all his trouble would be thrown away; but the knight paid no heed to them, and rode straight at the hill, and right up it, till he had gone two-thirds of the way, and then he wheeled his horse round and rode down again. To tell the truth, the *Princess* liked him still better than the knight in brass, and she sat and wished he might only be able to come right up to the top, and down the other side; but when she saw him turning back, she threw the second apple after him, and it rolled down and fell into his shoe. But, as soon as ever he had come down from the *Hill of Glass*, he rode off so fast that no one could see what became of him.

At even, when all were to go in before the king and the *Princess*, that he who had the golden apple might show it, in they went, one after the other, but there was no one who had any apple to show, and the two brothers, as they had done on the former day, went home and told how things had gone, and how all had ridden at the hill, and none got up.

"But, last of all," they said, "came one in a silver suit, and his horse had a silver saddle and a silver bridle. He was just a chap to ride; and he got two-thirds up the hill, and then turned back. He was a fine fellow, and no mistake; and the *Princess* threw the second gold apple to him."

"Oh!" said *Boots*, "I should so like to have seen him too, that I should."

"A pretty story," they said. "Perhaps you think his coat of mail was as bright as the ashes you are always poking about, and sifting, you nasty dirty beast."

The third day everything happened as it had happened the two days before. *Boots* begged to go and see the sight, but the two wouldn't hear of his going with them. When they got to the hill there was no one who could get so much as a yard up it; and now all waited for the knight in silver mail, but they neither saw nor heard of him. At last came one riding on a steed, so brave that no one had ever seen his match; and the knight had a suit of golden mail, and a golden saddle and bridle, so wondrous bright that the sunbeams gleamed from them a mile off. The other knights and princes could not find time to call out to him not to try his luck, for they were amazed to see how grand he was. So he rode right at the hill, and tore up it like nothing, so that the *Princess* hadn't even time to wish that he might get up the whole way. As soon as ever he reached the top, he took the third golden apple from the *Princess'* lap, and then turned his horse and rode down again. As soon as

But still the Horse begged him to look behind him. *Page* 156

he got down, he rode off at full speed, and was out of sight in no time.

Now, when the brothers got home at even, you may fancy what long stories they told, how the riding had gone off that day; and amongst other things, they had a deal to say about the knight in golden mail.

"He just was a chap to ride!" they said; "so grand a knight isn't to be found in the wide world."

"Oh!" said *Boots*, "I should so like to have seen him, that I should."

"Ah!" said his brothers, "his mail shone a deal brighter than the glowing coals which you are always poking and digging at; nasty dirty beast that you are."

Next day all the knights and princes were to pass before the king and the *Princess*—it was too late to do so the night before, I suppose—that he who had the gold apple might bring it forth; but one came after another, first the *Princes*, and then the knights, and still no one could show the gold apple.

"Well," said the king, "some one must have it, for it was something we all saw with our own eyes, how a man came and rode up and bore it off."

So he commanded that every man who was in the kingdom should come up to the palace and see if they could show the apple. Well, they all came one after another, but no one had the golden apple, and after a long time the two brothers of *Boots* came. They were the last of all, so the king asked them if there was no one else in the kingdom who hadn't come.

"Oh, yes," said they; "we have a brother, but he never carried off the golden apple. He hasn't stirred out of the dusthole on any of the three days."

"Never mind that," said the king; "he may as well come up to the palace like the rest."

So *Boots* had to go up to the palace.

"How now," said the king; "have you got the golden apple? Speak out!"

"Yes, I have," said *Boots;* "here is the first, and here is the second, and here is the third too;" and with that he pulled all three golden apples out of his pocket, and at the same time threw off his sooty rags, and stood before them in his gleaming golden mail.

"Yes!" said the king; "you shall have my daughter, and half my kingdom, for you well deserve both her and it."

So they got ready for the wedding, and *Boots* got the *Princess* to wife, and there was great merry-making at the bridal-feast, you may fancy, for they could all be merry though they couldn't ride up the *Hill of Glass*; and all I can say is, if they haven't left off their merry-making yet, why, they're still at it.

THE WIDOW'S SON

ONCE on a time there was a poor, poor *Widow*, who had an only *Son*. She dragged on with the boy till he had been confirmed, and then she said she couldn't feed him any longer, he must just go out and earn his own bread. So the lad wandered out into the world, and when he had walked a day or so, a strange man met him.

"Whither away?" asked the man.

"Oh, I'm going out into the world to try and get a place," said the lad.

"Will you come and serve me?" said the man.

"Oh, yes; just as soon you as any one else," said the lad.

"Well, you'll have a good place with me," said the man; "for you'll only have to keep me company, and do nothing at all else beside."

So the lad stopped with him, and lived on the fat of the land, both in meat and drink, and had little or nothing to do; but he never saw a living soul in that man's house.

So one day the man said:

"Now, I'm going off for eight days, and that time you'll have to spend here all alone; but you must not go into any one of these four rooms here. If you do, I'll take your life when I come back."

"No," said the lad, he'd be sure not to do that. But when the man had been gone three or four days, the lad couldn't bear it any longer, but went into the first room, and when he got inside he looked round, but he saw nothing but a shelf over the door where a bramble-bush rod lay.

Well, indeed! thought the lad; a pretty thing to forbid my seeing this.

So when the eight days were out, the man came home, and the first thing he said was:

"You haven't been into any of these rooms, of course."

"No, no; that I haven't," said the lad.

"I'll soon see that," said the man, and went at once into the room where the lad had been.

"Nay, but you have been in here," said he; "and now you shall lose your life."

Then the lad begged and prayed so hard that he got off with his life, but the man gave him a good thrashing.

And when it was over, they were as good friends as ever.

Some time after the man set off again, and said he should be away fourteen days; but before he went he forbade the lad to go into any of the rooms he had not been in before; as for that he had been in, he might go into that, and welcome. Well, it was the same story over again, except that the lad stood out eight days before he went in. In this room, too, he saw nothing but a shelf over the door, and a big stone, and a pitcher of water on it. Well, after all, there's not much to be afraid of my seeing here, thought the lad.

But when the man came back, he asked if he had been into any of the rooms. No, the lad hadn't done anything of the kind.

"Well, well; I'll soon see that," said the man; and when he saw the lad had been in them after all, he said:

"Ah! now I'll spare you no longer; now you must lose your life."

But the lad begged and prayed for himself again, and so this time too he got off with stripes; though he got as many as his skin would carry. But when he got sound and well again, he led just as easy a life as ever, and he and the man were just as good friends.

So a while after the man was to take another journey, and now he said he should be away three weeks, and he forbade the lad anew to go into the third room, for if he went in there he might just make up his mind at once to lose his life. Then after fourteen days the lad couldn't bear it, but crept into the room, but he saw nothing at all in there but a trap door on the floor; and when he lifted it up and looked down, there stood a great copper cauldron which bubbled up and boiled away down there; but he saw no fire under it.

"Well, I should just like to know if it's hot," thought the lad, and struck his finger down into the broth, and when he pulled it out again, lo! it was gilded all over. So the lad scraped and scrubbed it, but the gilding wouldn't go off, so he bound a piece of rag round it; and when the man came back, and asked what was the matter with his finger, the lad said he'd given it such a bad cut. But the man tore off the rag, and then he soon saw what was the matter with the finger. First he wanted to kill the lad outright, but when he wept, and begged, he only gave him such a thrashing that he had to keep his bed three days. After that the man took down a pot from the wall, and rubbed him over with

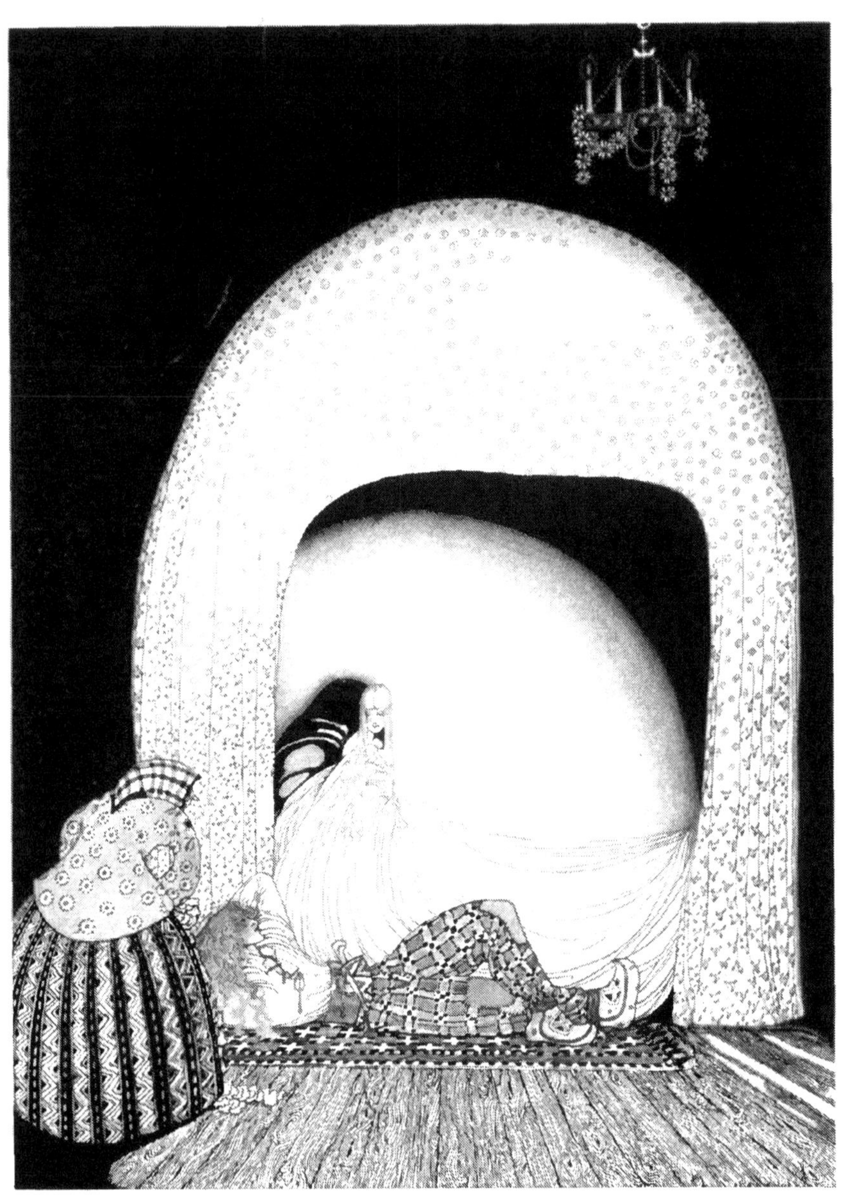

And this time she whisked off the wig; and there lay the lad, so lovely, and white and red, just as the Princess had seen him in the morning sun. Page 100

some stuff out of it, and so the lad was as sound and fresh as ever.

So after a while the man started off again, and this time he was to be away a month. But before he went, he said to the lad, if he went into the fourth room he might give up all hope of saving his life.

Well, the lad stood out for two or three weeks, but then he couldn't hold out any longer; he must and would go into that room, and so in he stole. There stood a great black horse tied up in a stall by himself, with a manger of red-hot coals at his head and a truss of hay at his tail. Then the lad thought this all wrong, so he changed them about, and put the hay at his head. Then said the *Horse:*

"Since you are so good at heart as to let me have some food, I'll set you free, that I will. For if the *Troll* comes back and finds you here, he'll kill you outright. But now you must go up to the room which lies just over this, and take a coat of mail out of those that hang there; and mind, whatever you do, don't take any of the bright ones, but the most rusty of all you see, that's the one to take; and sword and saddle you must choose for yourself just in the same way."

So the lad did all that; but it was a heavy load for him to carry them all down at once.

When he came back, the *Horse* told him to pull off his clothes and get into the cauldron which stood and boiled in the other room, and bathe himself there. "If I do," thought the lad, "I shall look an awful fright;" but for all that, he did as he was told. So when he had taken his bath, he became so handsome and sleek, and as red and white as milk and blood, and much stronger than he had been before.

"Do you feel any change?" asked the *Horse*.

"Yes," said the lad.

"Try and lift me, then," said the *Horse*.

Oh yes! he could do that, and as for the sword, he brandished it like a feather.

"Now saddle me," said the *Horse*, "and put on the coat of mail, and then take the bramble-bush rod, and the stone, and the pitcher of water, and the pot of ointment, and then we'll be off as fast as we can."

So when the lad had got on the horse, off they went at such a rate, he couldn't at all tell how they went. But when he had ridden awhile, the *Horse* said, "I think I hear a noise; look round! can you see anything?"

"Yes; there are ever so many coming after us, at least a score," said the lad.

"Aye, aye, that's the *Troll* coming," said the *Horse*; "now he's after us with his pack."

So they rode on a while, until those who followed were close behind them.

"Now throw your bramble-bush rod behind you, over your shoulder," said the *Horse;* "but mind you throw it a good way off my back."

So the lad did that, and all at once a close, thick bramblewood grew up behind them. So the lad rode on a long, long time, while the *Troll* and his crew had to go home to fetch something to hew their way through the wood. But at last the *Horse* said again.

"Look behind you! can you see anything now?"

"Yes, ever so many," said the lad, "as many as would fill a large church."

"Aye, aye, that's the *Troll* and his crew," said the *Horse;* "now he's got more to back him; but now throw down the stone, and mind you throw it far behind me."

And as soon as the lad did what the *Horse* said, up rose a great black hill of rock behind him. So the *Troll* had to be off home to fetch something to mine his way through the rock; and while the *Troll* did that, the lad rode a good bit further on. But still the *Horse* begged him to look behind him, and then he saw a troop like a whole army behind him, and they glistened in the sunbeams.

"Aye, aye," said the *Horse*, "that's the *Troll*, and now he's got his whole band with him, so throw the pitcher of water behind you, but mind you don't spill any of it upon me."

So the lad did that; but in spite of all the pains he took, he still spilt one drop on the horse's flank. So it became a great deep lake; and because of that one drop, the horse found himself far out in it, but still he swam safe to land. But when the *Trolls* came to the lake, they lay down to drink it dry; and so they swilled and swilled till they burst.

"Now we're rid of them," said the *Horse*.

So when they had gone a long, long while, they came to a green patch in a wood.

"Now, strip off all your arms," said the *Horse*, "and only put on your ragged clothes, and take the saddle off me, and let me loose, and hang all my clothing and your arms up inside that great hollow lime-tree yonder.

Then make yourself a wig of fir-moss, and go up to the king's palace, which lies close here, and ask for a place. Whenever you need me, only come here and shake the bridle, and I'll come to you."

Yes! the lad did all his *Horse* told him, and as soon as ever he put on the wig of moss he became so ugly, and pale, and miserable to look at, no one would have known him again. Then he went up to the king's palace and begged first for leave to be in the kitchen, and bring in wood and water for the cook, but then the kitchen-maid asked him:

"Why do you wear that ugly wig? Off with it. I won't have such a fright in here."

"No, I can't do that," said the lad; "for I'm not quite right in my head."

"Do you think then I'll have you in here about the food," cried the cook. "Away with you to the coachman; you're best fit to go and clean the stable."

But when the coachman begged him to take his wig off, he got the same answer, and he wouldn't have him either.

"You'd best go down to the gardener," said he; "you're best fit to go about and dig in the garden."

So he got leave to be with the gardener, but none of the other servants would sleep with him, and so he had to sleep by himself under the steps of the summer-house. It stood upon beams, and had a high staircase. Under that he got some turf for his bed, and there he lay as well as he could.

So, when he had been some time at the palace, it happened one morning, just as the sun rose, that the lad had taken off his wig, and stood and washed himself, and then he was so handsome, it was a joy to look at him.

So the *Princess* saw from her window the lovely gardener's boy, and thought she had never seen any one so handsome. Then she asked the gardener why he lay out there under the steps.

"Oh," said the gardener, "none of his fellow-servants will sleep with him; that's why."

"Let him come up to-night, and lie at the door inside my bedroom, and then they'll not refuse to sleep with him any more," said the *Princess*.

So the gardener told that to the lad.

"Do you think I'll do any such thing?" said the lad. "Why they'd say next there was something between me and the *Princess*."

"Yes," said the gardener, "you've good reason to fear any such thing, you who are so handsome."

"Well, well," said the lad, "since it's her will, I suppose I must go."

So, when he was to go up the steps in the evening, he tramped and stamped so on the way, that they had to beg him to tread softly lest the *King* should come to know it. So he came into the *Princess'* bedroom, lay down, and began to snore at once. Then the *Princess* said to her maid:

"Go gently, and just pull his wig off;" and she went up to him.

But just as she was going to whisk it off, he caught hold of it with both hands, and said she should never have it. After that he lay down again, and began to snore. Then the *Princess* gave her maid a wink, and this time she whisked off the wig; and there lay the lad so lovely, and white and red, just as the *Princess* had seen him in the morning sun.

After that the lad slept every night in the *Princess'* bedroom.

But it wasn't long before the *King* came to hear how the gardener's lad slept every night in the *Princess'* bedroom; and he got so wroth he almost took the lad's life. He didn't do that, however, but he threw him into the prison tower; and as for his daughter, he shut her up in her own room, whence she never got leave to stir day or night. All that she begged, and all that she prayed, for the lad and herself, was no good. The *King* was only more wroth than ever.

Some time after came a war and uproar in the land, and the *King* had to take up arms against another king who wished to take the kingdom from him. So when the lad heard that, he begged the gaoler to go to the *King* and ask for a coat of mail and a sword, and for leave to go to the war. All the rest laughed when the gaoler told his errand, and begged the *King* to let him

The Lad in the Battle. Page 161

have an old worn-out suit, that they might have the fun of seeing such a wretch in battle. So he got that, and an old broken-down hack besides, which went upon three legs, and dragged the fourth after it.

Then they went out to meet the foe; but they hadn't got far from the palace before the lad got stuck fast in a bog with his hack. There he sat and dug his spurs in, and cried, "Gee up! gee up!" to his hack. And all the rest had their fun out of this, and laughed, and made game of the lad as they rode past him. But they were scarcely gone, before he ran to the lime-tree, threw on his coat of mail, and shook the bridle, and there came the *Horse* in a trice, and said: "Do now your best, and I'll do mine."

But when the lad came up the battle had begun, and the *King* was in a sad pinch; but no sooner had the lad rushed into the thick of it than the foe was beaten back, and put to flight. The *King* and his men wondered and wondered who it could be who had come to help them, but none of them got so near him as to be able to talk to him, and as soon as the fight was over he was gone. When they went back, there sat the lad still in the bog, and dug his spurs into his three-legged hack, and they all laughed again.

"No! only just look," they said; "there the fool sits still."

The next day when they went out to battle, they saw the lad sitting there still, so they laughed again, and made game of him; but as soon as ever they had ridden by, the lad ran again to the lime-tree, and all happened as on the first day. Every one wondered what strange champion it could be that had helped them, but no one got so near him as to say a word to him; and no one guessed it could be the lad; that's easy to understand.

So when they went home at night, and saw the lad still sitting there on his hack, they burst out laughing at him again, and one of them shot an arrow at him and hit him in the leg. So he began to shriek and to bewail; 'twas enough to break one's heart; and so the *King* threw his pocket-handkerchief to him to bind his wound.

When they went out to battle the third day, the lad still sat there.

"Gee up! gee up!" he said to his hack.

"Nay, nay," said the *King's* men; "if he won't stick there till he's starved to death."

And then they rode on, and laughed at him till they were fit to fall from their horses. When they were gone, he ran again to the lime, and came up to the battle just in the very nick of time. This day he slew the enemy's king, and then the war was over at once.

When the battle was over, the *King* caught sight of his handkerchief, which the strange warrior had bound round his leg, and so it wasn't hard to find him out. So they took him with great joy between them to the palace, and the *Princess*, who saw him from her window, got so glad, no one can believe it.

"Here comes my own true love," she said.

Then he took the pot of ointment and rubbed himself on the leg, and after that he rubbed all the wounded, and so they all got well again in a moment.

So he got the *Princess* to wife; but when he went down into the stable where his horse was on the day the wedding was to be, there it stood so dull and heavy, and hung its ears down, and wouldn't eat its corn. So when the young *King*—for he was now a king, and had got half the kingdom—spoke to him, and asked what ailed him, the *Horse* said:

"Now I have helped you on, and now I won't live any longer. So just take the sword, and cut my head off."

"No, I'll do nothing of the kind," said the young *King*; "but you shall have all you want, and rest all your life."

"Well," said the *Horse*, "if you don't do as I tell you, see if I don't take your life somehow."

So the *King* had to do what he asked; but when he swung the sword and was to cut his head off, he was so sorry he turned away his face, for he would not see the stroke fall. But as soon as ever he had cut off the head, there stood the loveliest *Prince* on the spot where the horse had stood.

"Why, where in all the world did you come from?" asked the *King*.

"It was I who was a horse," said the *Prince*; "for I was king of that land whose king you slew yesterday. He it was who threw this *Troll's* shape over me, and sold me to the *Troll*. But now he is slain I get my own again, and you and I will be neighbour kings, but war we will never make on one another."

And they didn't either; for they were friends as long as they lived, and each paid the other very many visits.

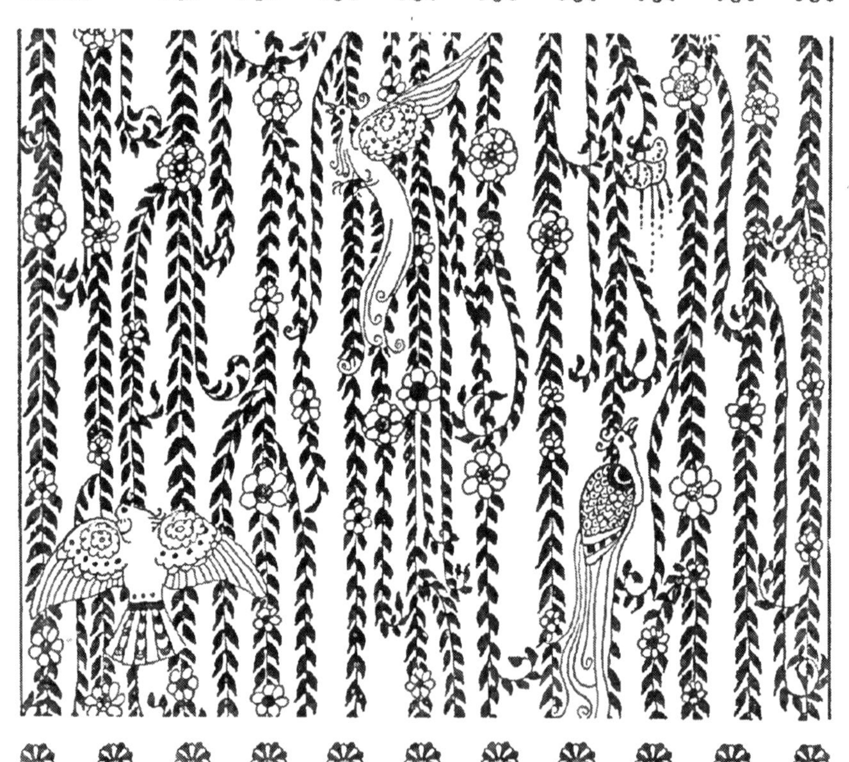

THE THREE BILLY-GOATS GRUFF

ONCE on a time there were three *Billy-goats*, who were to go up to the hill-side to make themselves fat, and the name of all three was "*Gruff*."

On the way up was a bridge over a burn they had to cross; and under the bridge lived a great ugly *Troll*, with eyes as big as saucers, and a nose as long as a poker.

So first of all came the youngest billy-goat *Gruff* to cross the bridge.

"Trip, trap! trip, trap!" went the bridge.

"WHO'S THAT tripping over my bridge?" roared the *Troll*.

"Oh! it is only I, the tiniest billy-goat *Gruff*; and I'm going up to the hill-side to make myself fat," said the billy-goat, with such a small voice.

"Now, I'm coming to gobble you up," said the *Troll.*

"Oh, no! pray don't take me. I'm too little, that I am," said the billy-goat; "wait a bit till the second billy-goat *Gruff* comes, he's much bigger."

"Well! be off with you," said the *Troll.*

A little while after came the second billy-goat *Gruff* to cross the bridge.

"TRIP, TRAP! TRIP, TRAP! TRIP, TRAP!" went the bridge.

"WHO'S THAT tripping over my bridge?" roared the *Troll.*

"Oh! it's the second billy-goat *Gruff*, and I'm going up to the hill-side to make myself fat," said the billy-goat, who hadn't such a small voice.

"Now, I'm coming to gobble you up," said the *Troll.*

"Oh, no! don't take me, wait a little till the big billy-goat *Gruff* comes, he's much bigger."

"Very well! be off with you," said the *Troll.*

But just then up came the big billy-goat *Gruff.*

"TRIP, TRAP! TRIP, TRAP! TRIP, TRAP!" went the bridge, for the billy-goat was so heavy that the bridge creaked and groaned under him.

Just as they bent down to take the rose a big dense snow-drift came and carried them away. Page 173

"WHO'S THAT tramping over my bridge?" roared the *Troll.*

"IT'S I! THE BIG BILLY-GOAT GRUFF," said the billy-goat, who had an ugly hoarse voice of his own.

"Now, I'm coming to gobble you up," roared the *Troll.*

"Well, come along! I've got two spears,
And I'll poke your eyeballs out at your ears;
I've got besides two curling-stones,
And I'll crush you to bits, body and bones."

That was what the big billy-goat said; and so he flew at the *Troll* and poked his eyes out with his horns, and crushed him to bits, body and bones, and tossed him out into the burn, and after that he went up to the hill-side. There the billy-goats got so fat they were scarce able to walk home again; and if the fat hasn't fallen off them, why they're still fat; and so:

Snip, snap, snout,
This tale's told out.

THE THREE PRINCESSES IN THE BLUE MOUNTAIN

THERE were once upon a time a *King* and *Queen* who had no children, and they took it so much to heart that they hardly ever had a happy moment. One day the *King* stood in the portico and looked out over the big meadows and all that was his. But he felt he could have no enjoyment out of it all, since he did not know what would become of it after his time. As he stood there pondering, an old beggar woman came up to him and asked him for a trifle in heaven's name. She greeted him and curtsied, and asked what ailed the *King*, since he looked so sad.

"You can't do anything to help me, my good woman," said the *King*; "it's no use telling you."

"I am not so sure about that," said the beggar woman. "Very little is wanted when luck is in the way. The *King* is thinking that he has no heir to his crown and kingdom, but he need not mourn on that account," she said. "The *Queen* shall have three daughters, but great care must be taken that they do not come out under the open heavens before they are all fifteen years old; otherwise a snowdrift will come and carry them away."

When the time came the *Queen* had a beautiful baby girl; the year after she had another, and the third year she also had a girl.

The *King* and *Queen* were glad beyond all measure; but although the *King* was very happy, he did not forget to set a watch at the Palace door, so that the *Princesses* should not get out.

As they grew up they became both fair and beautiful, and all went well with them in every way. Their only sorrow was that they were not allowed to go out and play like other children. For all they begged and prayed their parents, and for all they besought the sentinel, it was of no avail; go out they must not before they were fifteen years old, all of them.

So one day, not long before the fifteenth birthday of the youngest *Princess*, the *King* and the *Queen* were out driving, and the *Princesses* were standing at the window and looking out. The sun was shining, and everything looked so green and beautiful that they felt that they must go out, happen what might. So they begged and entreated and urged the sentinel, all three of them, that he should let them down into the garden. "He could see for himself how warm and pleasant it was; no snowy weather could come on such a day." Well, he didn't think it looked much like it either, and if they must go they had better go, the soldier said; but it must only be for a minute, and he himself would go with them and look after them.

When they got down into the garden they ran up and down, and filled their laps with flowers and green leaves, the prettiest they could find. At last they could manage no more, but just as they were going indoors they caught sight of a large rose at the other end of the garden. It was many times prettier than any they had gathered, so they must have that also. But just as they bent down to take the rose a big dense snowdrift came and carried them away.

There was great mourning over the whole country, and the *King* made known from all the churches that any one who could save the *Princesses* should have half the kingdom and his golden crown and whichever princess he liked to choose.

You can well understand there were plenty who wanted to gain half the kingdom, and a princess into the bargain; so there were people of both high and low degree who set out for all parts of the country. But there was no one who could find the *Princesses*, or even get any tidings of them.

When all the grand and rich people in the country had had their turn, a captain and a lieutenant came to the Palace, and wanted to try their luck. The *King* fitted them out both with silver and gold, and wished them success on their journey.

Then came a soldier, who lived with his mother in a little cottage some way from the Palace. He had dreamt one night that he also was trying to find the *Princesses*. When the morning came he still remembered what he had dreamt, and told his mother about it.

"Some witchery must have got hold of you," said the woman, "but you must dream the same thing three nights running, else there is nothing in it." And the next two nights the same thing happened; he had the same dream, and he felt he must go. So he washed himself and put on his uniform, and went into the kitchen at the Palace. It was the day after the captain and the lieutenant had set out.

"You had better go home again," said the *King*, "the *Princesses* are beyond your reach, I should say; and besides, I have spent so much money on outfits that I have nothing left to-day. You had better come back another time."

"If I go, I must go to-day," said the soldier. "Money I do not want; I only need a drop in my flask and some food in my wallet," he said; "but it must be a good walletful—as much meat and bacon as I can carry."

Yes, that he might have if that was all he wanted.

So he set off, and he had not gone many miles before he overtook the captain and the lieutenant.

"Where are you going?" asked the captain, when he saw the man in uniform.

"I'm going to try if I can find the *Princesses*," answered the soldier.

"So are we," said the captain, "and since your errand is the same, you may keep company with us, for if we don't find them, you are not likely to find them either, my lad," said he.

When they had gone awhile the soldier left the high road, and took a path into the forest.

"Where are you going?" said the captain; "it is best to follow the high road."

"That may be," said the soldier, "but this is my way."

He kept to the path, and when the others saw this they turned round and followed him. Away they went further and further, far across big moors and along narrow valleys.

And at last it became lighter, and when they had got out of the forest altogether they came to a long bridge, which they had to cross. But on that bridge a bear stood on guard. He rose on his hind legs and came towards them, as if he wanted to eat them.

"What shall we do now?" said the captain.

"They say that the bear is fond of meat," said the soldier, and then he threw a fore quarter to him, and so they got past. But when they reached the other end of the bridge, they saw a lion, which came roaring towards them with open jaws as if he wanted to swallow them.

"I think we had better turn right-about, we shall never be able to get past him alive," said the captain.

"Oh, I don't think he is so very dangerous," said the soldier; "I have heard that lions are very fond of bacon, and I have half a pig in my wallet;" and then he threw a ham to the lion, who began eating and gnawing, and thus they got past him also.

In the evening they came to a fine big house. Each room was more gorgeous than the other; all was glitter

The Troll was quite willing, and before long he fell asleep and began snoring. *Page 184*

and splendour wherever they looked; but that did not satisfy their hunger. The captain and the lieutenant went round rattling their money, and wanted to buy some food; but they saw no people nor could they find a crumb of anything in the house, so the soldier offered them some food from his wallet, which they were not too proud to accept, nor did they want any pressing. They helped themselves of what he had as if they had never tasted food before.

The next day the captain said they would have to go out shooting and try to get something to live upon. Close to the house was a large forest where there were plenty of hares and birds. The lieutenant was to remain at home and cook the remainder of the food in the soldier's wallet. In the meantime the captain and the soldier shot so much game that they were hardly able to carry it home. When they came to the door they found the lieutenant in such a terrible plight that he was scarcely able to open the door to them.

"What is the matter with you?" said the captain. The lieutenant then told them that as soon as they were gone a tiny, little man, with a long beard, who went on crutches, came in and asked so plaintively for a penny; but no sooner had he got it than he let it fall on the floor, and for all he raked and scraped with his crutch he was not able to get hold of it, so stiff and stark was he.

"I pitied the poor, old body," said the lieutenant, "and so I bent down to pick up the penny, but then he was neither stiff nor stark any longer. He began to belabour me with his crutches till very soon I was unable to move a limb."

"You ought to be ashamed of yourself! you, one of the king's officers, to let an old cripple give you a thrashing, and then tell people of it into the bargain!" said the captain. "Pshaw! to-morrow I'll stop at home, and then you'll hear another story."

The next day the lieutenant and the soldier went out shooting and the captain remained at home to do the cooking and look after the house. But if he fared no worse, he certainly fared no better than the lieutenant. In a little while the old man came in and asked for a penny. He let it fall as soon as he got it; gone it was and could not be found. So he asked the captain to help him to find it, and the captain, without giving a thought, bent down to look for it. But no sooner was he on his knees than the cripple began belabouring him with his crutches, and every time the captain tried to rise, he got a blow which sent him reeling. When the others came home in the evening, he still lay on the same spot and could neither see nor speak.

The third day the soldier was to remain at home, while the other two went out shooting. The captain said he must take care of himself, "for the old fellow will soon put an end to you, my lad," said he.

"Oh, there can't be much life in one if such an old crook can take it," said the soldier.

They were no sooner outside the door, than the old man came in and asked for a penny again.

"Money I have never owned," said the soldier, "but food I'll give you, as soon as it is ready," said he, "but if we are to get it cooked, you must go and cut the wood."

"That I can't," said the old man.

"If you can't, you must learn," said the soldier. "I will soon show you. Come along with me down to the wood-shed." There he dragged out a heavy log and cut a cleft in it, and drove in a wedge till the cleft deepened.

"Now you must lie down and look right along the cleft, and you'll soon learn how to cut wood," said the soldier.

"In the meantime I'll show you how to use the axe."

The old man was not sufficiently cunning, and did as he was told; he lay down and looked steadily along the log. When the soldier saw the old man's beard had got well into the cleft, he struck out the wedge; the cleft closed and the old man was caught by the beard. The soldier began to beat him with the axe handle, and then swung the axe round his head, and vowed that he would split his skull if he did not tell him, there and then, where the *Princesses* were.

"Spare my life, spare my life, and I'll tell you!" said the old man. "To the east of the house there is a big mound; on top of the mound you must dig out a square piece of turf, and then you will see a big stone slab. Under that there is a deep hole through which you must let yourself down, and you'll then come to another world where you will find the *Princesses*. But the way is long and dark and it goes both through fire and water."

When the soldier got to know this, he released the old man, who was not long in making off.

When the captain and lieutenant came home they were surprised to find the soldier alive. He told them what had happened from first to last, where the *Princesses* were and how they should find them. They became as pleased as if they had already found them, and when they had had some food, they took with them a basket and as much rope as they could find, and all three set off to the mound. There they first dug out the turf just as the old man had told them, and underneath they found a big stone slab, which it took all their strength to turn over. They then began to measure how deep it was; they joined on ropes both two and three times, but they were no nearer the bottom the last time than the first. At last they had to join all the ropes they had, both the coarse and fine, and then they found it reached the bottom.

The captain was, of course, the first who wanted to descend; "But when I tug at the rope you must make haste to drag me up again," he said. He found the way both dark and unpleasant, but he thought he would go on as long as it became no worse. But all at once he felt ice cold water spouting about his ears; he became frightened to death and began tugging at the rope.

The lieutenant was the next to try, but it fared no better with him. No sooner had he got through the flood of water than he saw a blazing fire yawning beneath him, which so frightened him that he also turned back.

The soldier then got into the bucket, and down he went through fire and water, right on till he came to the bottom, where it was so pitch dark that he could not see his hand before him. He dared not let go the basket, but went round in a circle, feeling and fumbling about him. At last he discovered a gleam of light far, far away like the dawn of day, and he went on in that direction.

When he had gone a bit it began to grow light around him, and before long he saw a golden sun rising in the sky and everything around him became as bright and beautiful as if in a fairy world.

First he came to some cattle, which were so fat that their hides glistened a long way off, and when he had got past them he came to a fine, big palace. He walked through many rooms without meeting anybody. At last he heard the hum of a spinning wheel, and when he entered the room he found the eldest *Princess* sitting there spinning copper yarn; the room and everything in it was of brightly polished copper.

"Oh, dear; oh, dear! what are Christian people doing here?" said the *Princess*. "Heaven preserve you! what do you want?"

"I want to set you free and get you out of the mountain," said the soldier.

"Pray do not stay. If the troll comes home he will put an end to you at once; he has three heads," said she.

"I do not care if he has four," said the soldier. "I am here, and here I shall remain."

"Well, if you will be so headstrong, I must see if I can help you," said the *Princess.*

She then told him to creep behind the big brewing-vat which stood in the front hall; meanwhile she would receive the troll and scratch his heads till he went to sleep.

"And when I go out and call the hens you must make haste and come in," she said. "But you must first try if you can swing the sword which is lying on the table." No, it was too heavy, he could not even move it. He had then to take a strengthening draught from the horn, which hung behind the door; after that he was just able to stir it, so he took another draught, and then he could lift it. At last he took a right, big draught, and he could swing the sword as easily as anything.

All at once the troll came home; he walked so heavily that the palace shook.

"Ugh, ugh! I smell Christian flesh and blood in my house," said he.

"Yes," answered the *Princess*, "a raven flew past here just now, and in his beak he had a human bone, which he dropped down the chimney; I threw it out and swept and cleaned up after it, but I suppose it still smells."

"So it does," said the troll.

"But come and lie down and I'll scratch your heads," said the *Princess*; "the smell will be gone by the time you wake."

The troll was quite willing, and before long he fell asleep and began snoring. When she saw he was sleeping soundly, she placed some stools and cushions under his heads and went to call the hens. The soldier then

As soon as they tugged at the rope, the Captain and the Lieutenant pulled up the Princesses, the one after the other. *Page 190*

stole into the room with the sword, and with one blow cut all the three heads off the troll.

The *Princess* was as pleased as a fiddler, and went with the soldier to her sisters, so that he could also set them free. First of all they went across a courtyard and then through many long rooms till they came to a big door.

"Here you must enter: here she is," said the *Princess*. When he opened the door he found himself in a large hall, where everything was of pure silver; there sat the second sister at a silver spinning-wheel.

"Oh, dear; oh, dear!" she said. "What do you want here?"

"I want to set you free from the troll," said the soldier.

"Pray do not stay, but go," said the *Princess*. "If he finds you here he will take your life on the spot."

"That would be awkward—that is if I don't take his first," said the soldier.

"Well, since you will stay," she said, "you will have to creep behind the big brewing-vat in the front hall. But you must make haste and come as soon as you hear me calling the hens."

First of all he had to try if he was able to swing the troll's sword, which lay on the table; it was much larger and heavier than the first one; he was hardly able to move it. He then took three draughts from the horn and he could then lift it, and when he had taken three more he could handle it as if it were a rolling pin.

Shortly afterwards he heard a heavy, rumbling noise that was quite terrible, and directly afterwards a troll with six heads came in.

"Ugh, ugh!" he said as soon as he got his noses inside the door. "I smell Christian blood and bone in my house."

"Yes, just think! A raven came flying past here with a thigh-bone, which he dropped down the chimney," said the *Princess.* "I threw it out, but the raven brought it back again. At last I got rid of it and made haste to clean the room, but I suppose the smell is not quite gone," she said.

"No, I can smell it well," said the troll; but he was tired and put his heads in the *Princess's* lap, and she went on scratching them till they all fell a-snoring. Then she called the hens, and the soldier came and cut off all the six heads as if they were set on cabbage stalks.

She was no less glad than her elder sister, as you may imagine, and danced and sang; but in the midst of their joy they remembered their youngest sister. They went with the soldier across a large courtyard, and, after walking through many, many rooms, he came to the hall of gold where the third sister was.

She sat at a golden spinning-wheel spinning gold yarn, and the room from ceiling to floor glistened and glittered till it hurt one's eyes.

"Heaven preserve both you and me, what do you want here?" said the *Princess*. "Go, go, else the troll will kill us both."

"Just as well two as one," answered the soldier. The *Princess* cried and wept; but it was all of no use, he must and would remain. Since there was no help for it he would have to try if he could use the troll's sword on the table in the front hall. But he was only just able to move it; it was still larger and heavier than the other two swords.

He then had to take the horn down from the wall and take three draughts from it, but was only just able to stir the sword. When he had taken three more draughts he could lift it, and when he had taken another three he

swung it as easily as if it had been a feather.

The *Princess* then settled with the soldier to do the same as her sisters had done. As soon as the troll was well asleep she would call the hens, and he must then make haste and come in and put an end to the troll.

All of a sudden they heard such a thundering, rambling noise, as if the walls and roof were tumbling in.

"Ugh! Ugh! I smell Christian blood and bone in my house," said the troll, sniffing with all his nine noses.

"Yes, you never saw the like! Just now a raven flew past here and dropped a human bone down the chimney. I threw it out, but the raven brought it back, and this went on for some time," said the *Princess;* but she got it buried at last, she said, and she had both swept and cleaned the place, but she supposed it still smelt.

"Yes, I can smell it well," said the troll.

"Come here and lie down in my lap and I will scratch your heads," said the *Princess*. "The smell will be all gone when you awake."

He did so, and when he was snoring at his best she put stools and cushions under the heads so that she could get away to call the hens. The soldier then came in in his stockinged feet and struck at the troll, so that eight of the heads fell off at one blow. But the sword was too short and did not reach far enough; the ninth head woke up and began to roar.

"Ugh! Ugh! I smell a Christian."

"Yes, here he is," answered the soldier, and before the troll could get up and seize hold of him the soldier struck him another blow and the last head rolled along the floor.

You can well imagine how glad the *Princesses* became now that they no longer had to sit and scratch the trolls' heads; they did not know how they could do enough for him who had saved them. The youngest *Princess* took off her gold ring and knotted it in his hair. They then took with them as much gold and silver as they thought they could carry and set off on their way home.

As soon as they tugged at the rope the captain and the lieutenant pulled up the *Princesses*, the one after the other. But when they were safely up, the soldier thought it was foolish of him not to have gone up before the *Princesses*, for he had not very much belief in his comrades. He thought he would first try them, so he put a heavy lump of gold in the basket and got out of the way. When the basket was half-way up they cut the rope and the lump of gold fell to the bottom with such a crash that the pieces flew about his ears.

"Now we are rid of him," they said, and threatened the *Princesses* with their life if they did not say that it was they who had saved them from the trolls. They were forced to agree to this, much against their will, and especially the youngest *Princess*; but life was precious, and so the two who were strongest had their way.

When the captain and lieutenant got home with the *Princesses* you may be sure there were great rejoicings at the palace. The *King* was so glad he didn't know which leg to stand on; he brought out his best wine from his cupboard and wished the two officers welcome. If they had never been honoured before they were honoured now in full measure, and no mistake. They walked and strutted about the whole of the day, as if they were the cocks of the walk, since they were now going to have the *King* for father-in-law. For it was understood they should each have whichever of the *Princesses* they liked and half the kingdom between them. They both wanted the youngest *Princess*, but for all they prayed and threatened her it was of no use; she would not hear or listen to either.

They then asked the *King* if they might have twelve men to watch over her; she was so sad and melancholy since she had been in the mountain that they were afraid she might do something to herself.

Yes, that they might have, and the *King* himself told the watch they must look well after her and follow her wherever she went and stood.

They then began to prepare for the wedding of the two eldest sisters; it should be such a wedding as never was heard or spoken of before, and there was no end to the brewing and the baking and the slaughtering.

In the meantime the soldier walked and strolled about down in the other world. He thought it was hard that he should see neither people nor daylight any more; but he would have to do something, he thought, and so for many days he went about from room to room and opened all the drawers and cupboards and searched about on the shelves and looked at all the fine things that were there. At last he came to a drawer in a table, in which there lay a golden key; he tried this key to all the locks he could find, but there was none it fitted till he came to a little cupboard over the bed, and in that he found an old rusty whistle. "I wonder if there is any sound in it," he thought, and put it to his mouth. No sooner had he whistled than he heard a whizzing and a whirring from all quarters, and such a large flock of birds swept down, that they blackened all the field in which they settled.

"What does our master want to-day?" they asked.

If he were their master, the soldier said, he would like to know if they could tell him how to get up to the earth again. No, none of them knew anything about that; "But our mother has not yet arrived," they said; "if she can't help you, no one can."

So he whistled once more, and shortly heard something flapping its wings far away, and then it began to blow so hard that he was carried away between the houses like a

No sooner had he whistled than he heard a whizzing and a whirring from all quarters, and such a large flock of birds swept down that they blackened all the field in which they settled. *Page 192*

wisp of hay across the courtyard, and if he had not caught hold of the fence he would no doubt have been blown away altogether.

A big eagle—bigger than you can imagine—then swooped down in front of him.

"You come rather sharply," said the soldier.

"As you whistle so I come," answered the eagle. So he asked her if she knew any means by which he could get away from the world in which they were.

"You can't get away from here unless you can fly," said the eagle, "but if you will slaughter twelve oxen for me, so that I can have a really good meal, I will try and help you. Have you got a knife?"

"No, but I have a sword," he said. When the eagle had swallowed the twelve oxen she asked the soldier to kill one more for victuals on the journey. "Every time I gape you must be quick and fling a piece into my mouth," she said, "else I shall not be able to carry you up to earth."

He did as she asked him and hung two large bags of meat round her neck and seated himself among her feathers. The eagle then began to flap her wings and off they went through the air like the wind. It was as much as the soldier could do to hold on, and it was with the greatest difficulty he managed to throw the pieces of flesh into the eagle's mouth every time she opened it.

At last the day began to dawn, and the eagle was then almost exhausted and began flapping with her wings, but the soldier was prepared and seized the last hind quarter and flung it to her. Then she gained strength and brought him up to earth. When she had sat and rested a while at the top of a large pine-tree she set off with him again at such a pace that flashes of lightning were seen both by sea and land wherever they went.

Close to the palace the soldier got off and the eagle flew home again, but first she told him that if he at any time should want her he need only blow the whistle and she would be there at once.

In the meantime everything was ready at the palace, and the time approached when the captain and lieutenant were to be married with the two eldest *Princesses*, who, however, were not much happier than their youngest sister; scarcely a day passed without weeping and mourning, and the nearer the wedding-day approached the more sorrowful did they become.

At last the *King* asked what was the matter with them; he thought it was very strange that they were not merry and happy now that they were saved and had been set free and were going to be married. They had to give some answer, and so the eldest sister said they never would be happy any more unless they could get such checkers as they had played with in the blue mountain.

That, thought the *King*, could be easily managed, and so he sent word to all the best and cleverest goldsmiths in the country that they should make these checkers for the *Princesses*. For all they tried there was no one who could make them. At last all the goldsmiths had been to the palace except one, and he was an old, infirm man who had not done any work for many years except odd jobs, by which he was just able to keep himself alive. To him the soldier went and asked to be apprenticed. The old man was so glad to get him, for he had not had an apprentice for many a day, that he brought out a flask from his chest and sat down to drink with the soldier. Before long the drink got into his head, and when the soldier saw this he persuaded him to go up to the palace and tell the *King* that he would undertake to make the checkers for the *Princesses*.

He was ready to do that on the spot; he had made finer and grander things in his day, he said. When the

King heard there was some one outside who could make the checkers he was not long in coming out.

"Is it true what you say, that you can make such checkers as my daughters want?" he asked.

"Yes, it is no lie," said the goldsmith; that he would answer for.

"That's well!" said the *King*. "Here is the gold to make them with; but if you do not succeed you will lose your life, since you have come and offered yourself, and they must be finished in three days."

The next morning when the goldsmith had slept off the effects of the drink, he was not quite so confident about the job. He wailed and wept and blew up his apprentice, who had got him into such a scrape while he was drunk. The best thing would be to make short work of himself at once, he said, for there could be no hope for his life; when the best and grandest goldsmiths could not make such checkers, was it likely that he could do it?

"Don't fret on that account," said the soldier, "but let me have the gold and I'll get the checkers ready in time; but I must have a room to myself to work in," he said. This he got, and thanks into the bargain.

The time wore on, and the soldier did nothing but lounge about, and the goldsmith began to grumble, because he would not begin with the work.

"Don't worry yourself about it," said the soldier, "there is plenty of time! If you are not satisfied with what I have promised you had better make them yourself." The same thing went on both that day and the next; and when the smith heard neither hammer nor file from the soldier's room the whole of the last day, he quite gave himself up for lost; it was now no use to think any longer about saving his life, he thought.

But when the night came on the soldier opened the window and blew his whistle. The eagle then came and asked what he wanted.

"Those gold checkers, which the *Princesses* had in the blue mountain," said the soldier; "but you'll want something to eat first, I suppose? I have two ox carcases lying ready for you in the hay-loft yonder; you had better finish them," he said. When the eagle had done she did not tarry, and long before the sun rose she was back again with the checkers. The soldier then put them under his bed and lay down to sleep.

Early next morning the goldsmith came and knocked at his door.

"What are you after now again?" asked the soldier. "You rush about enough in the day, goodness knows! If one cannot have peace when one is in bed, whoever would be an apprentice here?" said he.

Neither praying nor begging helped that time; the goldsmith must and would come in, and at last he was let in.

And then, you may be sure, there was soon an end to his wailing.

But still more glad than the goldsmith were the *Princesses*, when he came up to the palace with the checkers, and gladdest of all was the youngest *Princess*.

"Have you made them yourself?" she asked.

"No, if I must speak the truth, it is not I," he said, "but my apprentice, who has made them."

"I should like to see that apprentice," said the *Princess*. In fact all three wanted to see him, and if he valued his life, he would have to come.

He was not afraid, either of women-folk or grand-folk, said the soldier, and if it could be any amusement to them to look at his rags, they should soon have that pleasure.

The youngest *Princess* recognised him at once; she pushed the soldiers aside and ran up to him, gave him her hand, and said:

"Good day, and many thanks for all you have done for us. It is he who freed us from the trolls in the mountain," she said to the *King*. "He is the one I will have!" and then she pulled off his cap and showed them the ring she had tied in his hair.

It soon came out how the captain and lieutenant had behaved, and so they had to pay the penalty of their treachery with their lives, and that was the end of their grandeur. But the soldier got the golden crown and half the kingdom, and married the youngest *Princess*.

At the wedding they drank and feasted both well and long; for feast they all could, even if they could not find the *Princesses*, and if they have not yet done feasting and drinking they must be at it still.

THE CAT ON THE DOVREFELL

ONCE on a time there was a man up in Finnmark who had caught a great white bear, which he was going to take to the King of Denmark. Now, it so fell out, that he came to the *Dovrefell* just about Christmas Eve, and there he turned into a cottage where a man lived, whose name was Halvor, and asked the man if he could get house-room there for his bear and himself.

"Heaven never help me, if what I say isn't true!" said the man; "but we can't give anyone house-room just now, for every Christmas Eve such a pack of *Trolls* come down upon us, that we are forced to flit, and haven't so much as a house over our own heads, to say nothing of lending one to anyone else."

"Oh?" said the man, "if that's all, you can very well lend me your house; my bear can lie under the stove yonder, and I can sleep in the side-room."

Well, he begged so hard, that at last he got leave to stay there; so the people of the house flitted out, and before they went, everything was got ready for the *Trolls*;

the tables were laid, and there was rice porridge, and fish boiled in lye, and sausages, and all else that was good, just as for any other grand feast.

So, when everything was ready, down came the *Trolls*. Some were great, and some were small; some had long tails, and some had no tails at all; some, too, had long, long noses; and they ate and drank, and tasted everything. Just then one of the little *Trolls* caught sight of the white bear, who lay under the stove; so he took a piece of sausage and stuck it on a fork, and went and poked it up against the bear's nose, screaming out:

"Pussy, will you have some sausage?"

Then the white bear rose up and growled, and hunted the whole pack of them out of doors, both great and small.

Next year Halvor was out in the wood, on the afternoon of Christmas Eve, cutting wood before the holidays, for he thought the *Trolls* would come again; and just as he was hard at work, he heard a voice in the wood calling out:

"Halvor! Halvor!"

"Well," said Halvor, "here I am."

"Have you got your big cat with you still?"

"Yes, that I have," said Halvor; "she's lying at home under the stove, and what's more, she has now got seven kittens, far bigger and fiercer than she is herself."

"Oh, then, we'll never come to see you again," bawled out the *Troll* away in the wood, and he kept his word; for since that time the *Trolls* have never eaten their Christmas brose with Halvor on the *Dovrefell*.

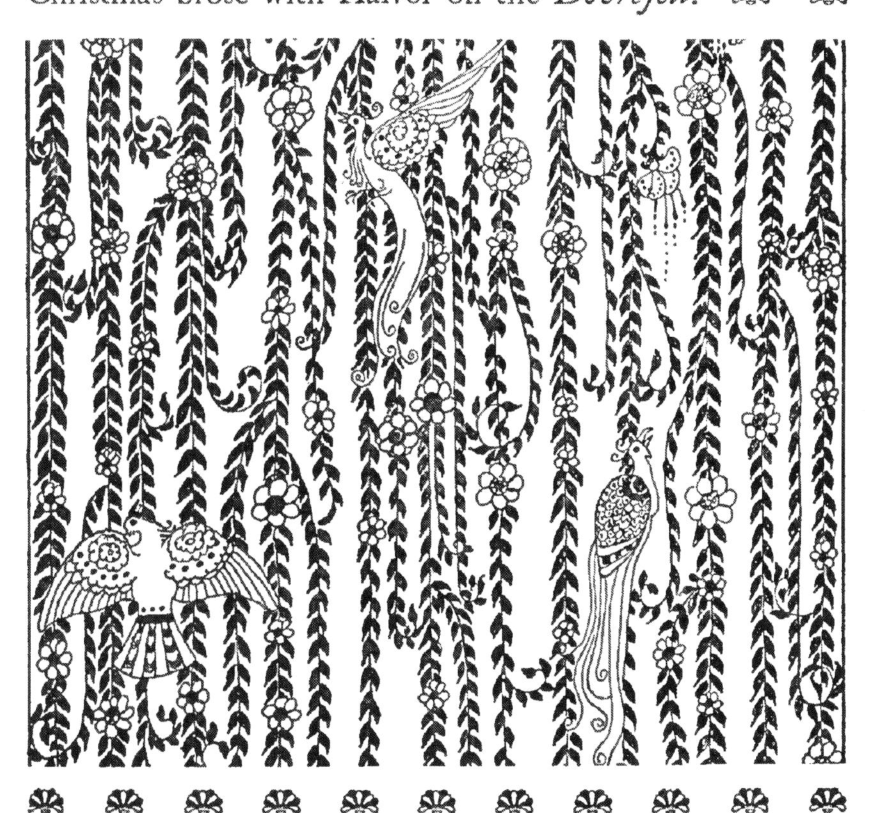

ONE'S OWN CHILDREN ARE ALWAYS PRETTIEST

A SPORTSMAN went out once into a wood to shoot, and he met a *Snipe*.

"Dear friend," said the *Snipe*, "don't shoot my children!"

"How shall I know your children?" asked the *Sportsman*. "What are they like?"

"Oh!" said the *Snipe*, "mine are the prettiest children in all the wood."

"Very well," said the *Sportsman*, "I'll not shoot them; don't be afraid."

But for all that, when he came back, there he had a whole

string of young snipes in his hand which he had shot.

"Oh, oh!" said the *Snipe*, "why did you shoot my children after all?"

"What! these your children!" said the *Sportsman*; "why, I shot the ugliest I could find, that I did!"

"Woe is me!" said the *Snipe*; "don't you know that each one thinks his own children the prettiest in the world?"

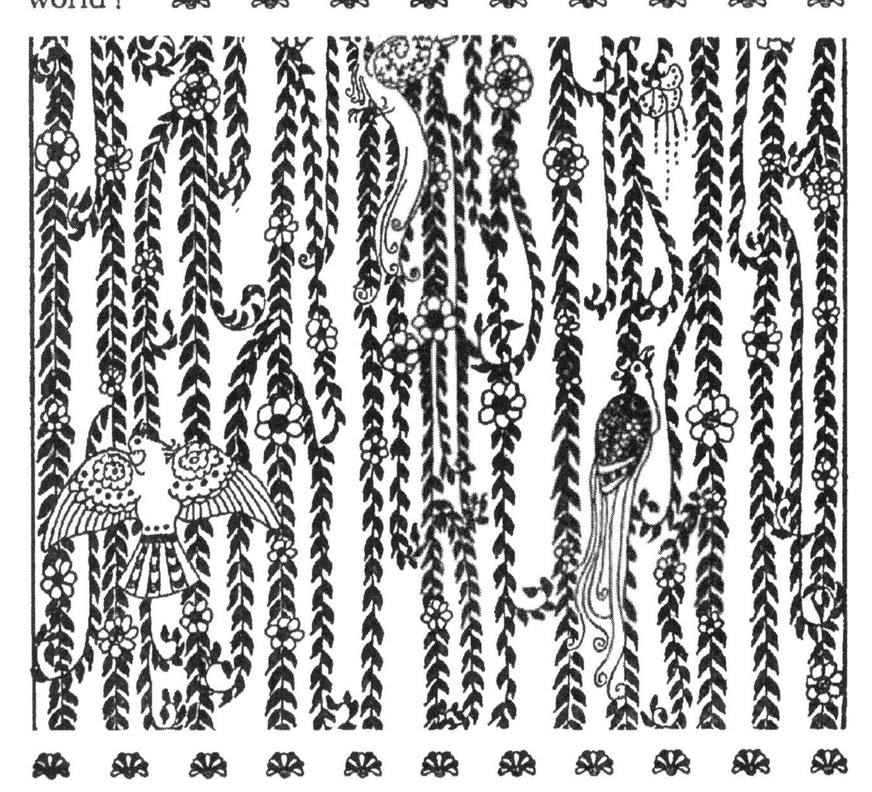

Milton Keynes UK
Ingram Content Group UK Ltd.
UKHW050009060124
435443UK00004BA/97